04/06

d.6

And all life on earth

dies

Also by Margaret Bechard

Hanging On to Max

SPACER

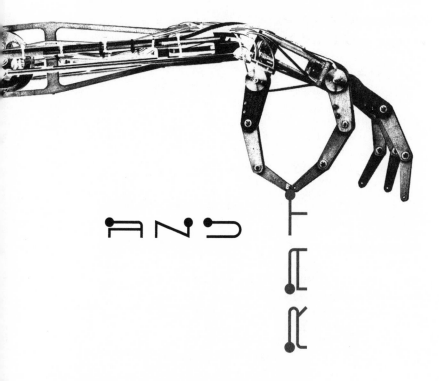

AND RAT

Margaret Bechard

A Deborah Brodie Book • ROARING BROOK PRESS • New Milford, Connecticut

A Deborah Brodie Book
Published by Roaring Brook Press
Roaring Brook Press is a division of Holtzbrinck Publishing Holdings
Limited Partnership
143 West Street, New Milford, Connecticut 06776

Library of Congress Cataloging-in-Publication Data

Bechard, Margaret.
    Spacer and Rat / Margaret Bechard.
        p. cm.
    "A Deborah Brodie book."
    Summary: Jack's predictable existence on Freedom space station is trans-
formed when Kit, the Earthie rat, enters his life and enlists him and a sensi-
tive robot in an effort to outwit the Company.
    ISBN 1-59643-058-3
    [1. Science fiction.]   I. Title.
    PZ7.B38066Sp 2005
    [Fic]—dc22   2004027670

Roaring Brook Press books are available for special promotions and
premiums. For details, contact: Director of Special Markets, Holtzbrinck
Publishers

Book design by Patti Ratchford
Printed in the United States of America
First edition October 2005

ACKNOWLEDGMENTS

Some books write themselves. Some books take a village.

This book took a small city, including the suburbs and outlying areas.

Both of my critique groups heard many, many versions of these chapters as I bumbled my way around the Asteroid Belt. Their insightful comments and critiques were always helpful. Their eagerness to know "what happens next" kept me working.

My editor, Deborah Brodie, asked the right questions to keep me focused on my characters and their story. She also generously and patiently ignored my many neurotic outbursts. If I were going to design an ideal editor, she would be the model.

Large parts of this story belong to my family. My husband, Lee, spent hours with his physics texts and his calculator, designing space stations and spaceships and computing travel times. My youngest son, Peter—who planted the seed for this story when he said, "You know what every pirate needs? A GPS!"—contributed enthusiastically to many dinner-table discussions of rocket propulsion and space-station design and artificial intelligence. My middle son, Nicholas, talked to me about the composition of asteroids and the potential for mining in outer space and told me I should really try listening to The Flaming Lips. My oldest son, Alex, helped me search for quotations in Shakespeare, did a thorough reading of a final draft, and left me helpful notes on my bulletin board. (Sorry, Alex, I could not work in the magical pony. Maybe next time.) All four of them read early drafts and pointed out my errors with humor and sensitivity. Most important were their unflagging enthusiasm and interest and their willingness to answer any question, no matter how inane. The good ideas in the story belong to them. The mistakes that remain are all my own.

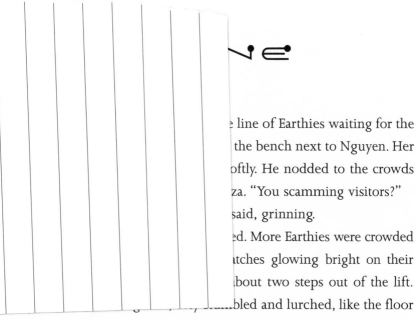

line of Earthies waiting for the
the bench next to Nguyen. Her
oftly. He nodded to the crowds
za. "You scamming visitors?"
said, grinning.
ed. More Earthies were crowded
itches glowing bright on their
bout two steps out of the lift.
bled and lurched, like the floor
of the station had risen up and knocked them back.

Nguyen clapped her hands and laughed. "Welcome to
Freedom Station!" she shouted.

Jack laughed, too. The drop from zero gee at the shuttle
dock to the full grav of the station had to be a shocker.
Probably the worst part of their trip out to the Belt. He shook
his head. "I just love the looks on their faces. They are so surprised. Like they thought they were stepping out onto Earth."

"They'll learn," Nguyen said. She made an adjustment
to the board, and the red bishop shouted an insult at the
black queen.

"Nice piece of tech," Jack said. "Did you make the
changes yourself?"

"Nothing illegal," Nguyen said, loud and clear. Just in
case there was a Company spook lurking nearby, taking

notes. "Just made the game a little more interesting." The black pawns started sharpening their swords. Nguyen leaned back on the bench. "What brings you to the North Dock anyway? Gert close the pub early today?"

"That'll happen when the sun burns out." Jack patted the sling bag, dangling fat and heavy from his right shoulder. "I had to pick up a delivery from Red Vera, and I thought I'd check out the arrivals. See who's coming to celebrate Perihelion. Leo's supposed to come in from the Shipyard today. And Tranh."

"And Annie," Nguyen said, grinning again.

"And Annie," Jack said. He wanted to find her as soon as she came back on-station. He wanted her to be the first to know.

There was a commotion in the baggage line. Two security guards had grabbed an Earthie bound for Ganymede and were demanding to search his bags. All bags got searched, ever since a group of colonists had smuggled eight cats on-station. And their cryo boxes had thawed early.

"You missed all the excitement," Nguyen said. "A group of New Oslo colonists got off the right lift just as a Pallas bunch got off the left. They started fighting it out, right in the middle of the plaza. It was stellar."

"Dailies said today the O-two explosion on New Oslo was a confirmed assassination attempt," Jack said. "They're blaming it on Pallan extremists."

Nguyen shook her head. "Half the colony worlds aren't worth living on, let alone fighting over."

"Better than Earth, though," Jack said. He watched the new group of Earthies stagger over to the end of the DNA line. He could smell them. Quarantine spray and disinfectant soap and something harsh and bitter. Something he always thought of as Earth itself. "Gert said there's another famine somewhere. That's why so many of them are coming out here now."

A sci guy, on leave from Saturn's moons, stopped in front of them. He nodded at Jack. "You playing, kid, or just using up atmo?"

"Just leaving," Jack said. He stood up. Nguyen was already bending over the board.

Jack circled around past the info sign. The Armstrong holo was out, reciting the station regs. Some spacer had hacked it the week before. After "No excess use of station resources," there was a faint click. Now the old astronaut tipped his clumsy, helmeted head and said, "Remember, visitors. In space, no one can hear you whine."

The head tip was an especially nice touch, Jack thought.

A little flock of maintenance bots was hovering in midair in front of the holo, their laser drivers and memory probes extended. As Jack passed, they swiveled their optics toward him. "Maintenance has arrived," they chorused in their flat, tinny voices.

"Then get to work," Jack said. He'd take bots over Earthies any day. Bots couldn't whine.

The left lift opened.

A group of geeks from the satellite array and some sci guys stepped out. Followed by Annie and her father. Annie's father headed for the workers' check-in line. She shouldered both their duffels and pushed her way over to an empty bench.

Jack watched her, craning around the crowd to keep her in sight. Annie had been working off-station, out in the Shipyard for one whole cycle. One whole cycle plus three weeks. Not that anybody had been counting.

"Get your hot sweet potatoes!" Veggie Tom stopped his barrow bot next to Armstrong. When he turned toward a family of Earthies, Jack snatched a potato piece out of the hot pot.

Annie's face lit up with a big smile when he stopped in front of her bench.

"Welcome home." He held out the potato, warm and steamy.

"Thanks!" She took a bite. "Oh, Pluto, that's good." She closed her eyes, briefly, and heaved a sigh. "We've been living on nutricubes for the past week."

She scooted over, and Jack sat down next to her. "So, other than the food, how's working in the Yard?"

She finished off the potato and licked her fingers. They were flecked with rosin stains, dark against her coppery skin. "It is absolutely flash. I mean, way better than I expected." She sighed again, deeper, happier, and flicked back her long black hair. She'd already braided a strand of yellow

Perihelion beads down the side. "I've been disassembling thrusters, grunt work of course, but mostly in zero gee. And yesterday they let me do a pressure check on a Zephyr-class. All by myself."

No surprise Annie was apprenticed to the mech crew. Before she could even talk, she'd been taking apart the vid players in the Nursery. Drove all the nannies loony. "You're a natural, Annie." And from the look on her face, Jack knew he'd said the right thing.

"How's your work? How's the pub?"

"Oh. The pub is totally flash. Last week? Gert let me change the synale tap." He raised his eyebrows. "All by myself."

Annie laughed. "You're going to be busy, too. All these workers coming on-station for the holiday. Not to mention all these Earthies."

He couldn't hold it in anymore. "I got the job, Annie."

"The what?"

"The job? Remember, the food-service posting in the dailies? I got the job on Liberty Station!"

"True fact?" She turned all the way toward him. "When did you find out?"

"Yesterday. I got a bounce yesterday from the Company offices."

"And have you heard from your mother's brother? Is he really out there?"

Only Annie knew he'd been searching the Company

archives. Looking for family. Jack frowned. "He's out there. DNA files confirmed it. But, you know, I'm going to wait. Until I get there. Until I can actually meet him and his kids."

"Cousins," Annie said.

"What?"

"It's an old word. It's what they used to call the off-spring of your parents' siblings."

"No kidding." Jack would have to remember that.

"So when do you leave?"

"I transfer next cycle."

"Wow. Next cycle. That's really soon." A look flashed across her face. But it was gone almost before Jack saw it.

"It'll really be midcycle," he said. "More like forty-five days. I catch passage out on the freighter *Isaac Asimov*." He was grinning again. "It's going to be completely stellar, Annie. The job's going to be much better. Liberty gets all the big ore transports and the experimental expeditions. And, you won't believe this. Because it's so close to the ore asteroids, you can rent a zip scooter and mining equipment. So I'll be able to go prospecting. You know, on my days off." He could maybe take those kids. Those cousins. "Asteroid hopping on a zip scooter. How flash is that?"

"I don't know, Jack." Annie laughed. "I kind of can't see you on a scooter."

"What do you mean?" He held his hands out in front of him, like he was grabbing the controls on a scooter's handle-bars. "Your dad let me drive last time I went off-station with him. Turns out I'm a natural." Jack imitated the swoop of a scooter, leaning right, then left. His shoulder bumped into Annie's.

She bumped him back, hard enough to push him into the arm of the bench. A guard pacing by shot them a suspicious look.

Annie straightened up. "So now there are two good reasons to have the party."

Jack straightened up, too. "The party?"

Annie sighed and whipped her hair back again. "Don't tell me you've forgotten the party, helium head."

"No. No. Of course not." But he had. As soon as he'd gotten word about Liberty, he'd pretty much forgotten about everything else.

"I've been bouncing with Nguyen and Luna. We've got it all planned." Annie frowned. "Well, almost all planned. We've still gotta find a place. But it's going to be the best Perihelion party yet." Her frown cleared, and she rested her hand on Jack's leg. "And I am glad about Liberty. I know how much you've wanted this."

"Thanks," Jack said. Although all he could think about, right then, was her hand, warm and heavy, on his leg.

The chron above the Company offices chimed the hour. "Oh, spam." Jack hoisted the sling bag up onto his shoulder. "I gotta get this stuff to Gert."

Annie's hand slipped away. "Does she know you're quitting?"

"The Company notified her. She's already been down to the Nursery, checking out the next batch of apprentices. And I'm not quitting." Jack stretched the word out. "I'm being transferred."

"Right," Annie said. "Well, as soon as I know the party data, I'll bounce you a vocal off the grid."

Jack stood up. "Stellar." And he meant it. For the first Perihelion in a long time, he really felt like partying.

He caught the tram heading to the Workers' Sector and found a seat at the back of the trailer. Two klicks above, the station overheads were already starting to dim, slowly switching from day to night. The tram left the plaza and started down the main street. Past the Company offices and the guard headquarters. The only buildings two stories tall on all of Freedom. Wiper bots were busy at all the windows, and polishers were waxing the walls. But no matter how hard they scrubbed, the buildings always looked gray and blank to Jack.

He leaned back against the trailer's railing and thought about Annie and her father, catching the next tram. Going over to the Infirmary to get Annie's mom at her clinic. Going back to their quarters together. And he imagined, again, how it might be on Liberty.

He hopped out at Grissom. A group of Earthies blocked the sidewalk, arguing about the best way to get to the Visitors' Sector. They looked at Jack hopefully. Came all the way out to the Black and got lost just trying to get around

Freedom. Jack dodged past them without speaking and headed down the alley.

The lights were coming on over the shop doors. The paint on the buildings wasn't so fresh and shiny. No bots were wiping and polishing. And the floor tile in front of Tariq's Wafer Shack was still cracked and curling up. Two farmers were coming out of Ollie's with their dinners. Across from Gert's, the usual sci guys were standing outside Madame Io's, watching the naked holos.

Jack stopped beside the fence that ran around the pub's side yard. The inorganics recycler was humming, processing a load of Gert's empties. A cool breeze fanned up from the South Dock. Cycle Four of the weather program. Jack took a deep breath and caught the smell of the fish farm, heavy and musty. Gert would say it was the ventilation glitching again. Gert would say the Company admins should get off their big, soft, fat butts and fix a few things around here.

But Jack had always kind of liked that smell.

Over the soft drone of the recycler, he heard a thump. And then a bump.

Slowly, carefully, Jack set down the sling bag and peered over the fence.

A rat was sneaking out from behind the bin of the recycler.

"Hey!" Jack shouted. "Hey!"

The rat froze. Its head turned, and just for a nano, it stared up at Jack.

And then it made a dash for freedom.

"No!" Jack leapt over the sling bag. He reached the gate just as the rat did. His fingers hooked into its shirt collar. "Got you!"

A booted foot shot out and whacked him, hard, on the knee.

"Ow! Ow! Drekking . . . ow!"

"Let me go," the rat hissed. "Let me go, you toxic spacer!" The foot shot out again.

Jack jumped back, lost his grip on the collar, and barely managed to grab the rat's sleeve.

And realized it was a girl. Spam. Girl rats were the worst. They cried. They whined.

"You some kind of perv?" the rat said. And she slapped him, hard, right across the face.

Jack let go of her and rubbed his cheek. "Jupiter's eye. You don't have to hit people, you dim rat."

The Earthie girl glared at him, her hands on her hips, all wild, wiry white hair and eyes as bright green and iridescent as fish scales. They had to be gen mods, no way they could be natural, but Jack had never seen them in the catalog. "You don't have to grab people." She sounded just like a school vid, teaching the basic regs. "And don't call me 'rat.'"

Jack laughed. "You are a rat. True fact. Your parents dumped you here."

"Look, spacer." She took a step closer, her eyes narrow bright slits. Jack took a step back. He couldn't help it. "No one dumped me on this rusty space station."

It happened all the time. Earthie parents got out this far into the Black and ran out of supplies, ran out of credit. Ran out of caring. They knew the guards would round their kids up and shuttle them right back to Earth.

Jack and Annie, Nguyen and Eli and Rigel, they'd had some stellar rat hunts, when they were kids. There were lots of games you could play with rats, before you turned them over to the guards.

This rat stood up straighter. She could almost look him in the eye. "I'm here to refit and resupply." She frowned, and her hand tightened on the small duffel she had over one shoulder. "And to arrange transport into the Belt," she added.

Not just a rat, but clearly dysfunctional. Not really a rat to play games with. "You know what?" Jack said. "You can just tell all this spam to the guards."

The door to the pub rattled open. "Jack!" Gert roared.

"I'm right here!" he shouted, glancing back. "I've caught a—"

His hand closed on thin air. He spun around.

The rat was already across the yard and up onto the fence. She glanced back once.

And smiled.

"Hey!"

She was over the top and gone. There was nothing left but the sharp whiff of Earth.

TWO

GERT WAS already back behind the bar when Jack walked into the pub. "You go all the way out to the Junkyard, boy?" she snapped.

Booker John shook his head sadly. The actor was sitting on his regular stool at the end of the bar. Where he could stretch out his legs. "I'll tell you, Jack. Gert here's been just about run off her feet."

Jack checked around the room. A couple of farmers playing the Home Port game in the corner. Two miners on the front couch. A tinjock slumped on the stool near the wall. "Yeah. It must have been chaos in here." He set the bag down on the bar. "I had to wait for Red Vera's guy to show up." True fact.

Gert glanced down the bar, but the tinjock hadn't even lifted her head. Gert lowered her voice anyway. "Red Vera and her crew hijacked the *Dan Simmons* just off Phobos two cycles ago," she said to Booker John. She opened up a cryo can and picked up the sling bag. "Freighter was heavy-loaded with special-order food and drink. For the Company admins." She poured the coffee beans into the can and sealed it tight. She winked her green eye at Booker John.

"At least the rakers are keeping the economy healthy." Booker John took a sip of his whiskey. "Were there a lot of new arrivals at the dock, Jack?"

"Plaza's packed with Earthies. They must be running double shuttles from Quarantine." Jack did the figures, quick, in his head. "Must be over a hundred just this past week. I even saw a rat. In the recycler yard."

"You catch it?" Gert turned, her hands on her hips. "We don't want them using up station resources."

"She . . . it was already going over the fence. When I saw it." Jack crossed to the sink, which was overflowing with dirty dishes. He got out the scrub bots.

"Drekking Earthies," Gert said.

"It must be frightening, though," Booker John said. "To be out here in the Black all alone. Poor little rat."

Jack turned and looked at him. His knee still throbbed where her boot had hit. "This rat wasn't that little," he said.

"Drekking Earthies," Gert said again. "If they're not trying to kill each other, they're dumping their kids for somebody else to worry about." She leaned over and poured a refill for the tinjock and another for Booker John. "They ruined Earth and now they're going to ruin the rest of the solar system."

"Should leave space to the spacers," Booker John said.

"Too drekking right." Gert set the whiskey bottle down with a clunk. "And guess who else can't stay buttoned up where he belongs? Guess who else has decided he has to go touring around the system?"

Jack rolled his eyes. You'd think he'd announced he was joining a colony.

"Jack?" Booker John put down his drink to study him. "You're leaving Freedom?"

"He's got plans," Gert said. Same way she'd say he'd caught a fungus.

"The Company is transferring me," Jack said. "There's an opening in one of the restaurants on Liberty Station." He wasn't going to mention his mother's brother. He knew what Gert would say about that.

"Restaurant." Gert tugged at a clump of her short gray hair. "Glorified noodle barrow is more like it."

Booker John was leaning back on his stool, his light brown eyes bright in his dark face. "Is it the Douglas Adams Eatery? Is that where you'll be working?"

Jack nodded. "Yeah. That's right. They call it the restaurant at the end of the Asteroid Belt." He liked the way that sounded. The end of the Asteroid Belt.

Booker John smiled. "It's one of my favorite places in the whole system. I had a cassoulet there once—totally recycled, mind you—that I've never forgotten." He caught Gert's eye. "Not that it could compare to your chowder, Gert. No comparison is possible." Booker John pointed at Jack. "Of course, you will get a better class of customers out there closer to Jupiter." His shaggy eyebrows waggled up and down. "Better tips, too."

First chance he got, Jack would scan the grid for *cassoulet*. "The current owner's almost retirement grade, too. So I've got a good chance of running the place myself. Maybe in less than an orbit." A better job in a better place. With people he maybe even belonged to.

"Oh." Gert folded her arms across her chest. "Now, that I'd like to see. You running a restaurant."

"Are you saying he hasn't gotten the proper training here, Gert?" Booker John asked. And his eyes were big and wide and innocent.

And Gert opened her mouth, then shut it.

Jack grinned. Only Booker John could do that to Gert.

The door opened, and two more farmers, their boots still wet from the ponic tanks, came in. "Synale and chowder, Gert!" they both shouted.

"Take a seat!" Gert pointed to an empty table and then jabbed Jack, hard, in the chest. "And you, don't forget you're still working for me. So clear those tables and get me some clean dishes."

Jack cleared the tables and dumped the new load of dishes into the sink on top of the bots. One of the miners dropped a trade chip in the juke bot. It started wailing out "Around We Go Again."

Booker John groaned. "Ah, the sweet, sweet song of Perihelion. Definitely time for me to go." He drained his glass and stood up, stretching to his full height. Two meters, easy. Jack didn't know if it was a gen mod or just the effects of lower grav. "Curtain's up in an hour," Booker John said. "You should try to catch our show, Jack."

"What play are you doing?"

"One of the best." Booker John flipped his long braid back over his shoulder and dug into the pocket of his faded orange coverall. He pulled out an ad wafer and set it on the bar. The holo sprang up automatically. A little Booker John and a woman, both dressed in something out of a history vid, stepped toward Jack. "Macbeth," the holo Booker John said. "Murder, mayhem"—the woman slid her arm through his—"and treachery." She smiled. "Shows daily 2000 hours," she added. "Public Meeting Hall 6. Visitors' Sector." The holo sparked once and faded.

Booker John had a long face, and the corners of his eyes always drooped down. But when he smiled, like now, every-thing lifted and lightened. Like he was floating in zero gee. He crooked a finger, and Jack leaned forward. "We added three totally gratuitous laser blade fights and a tasteful sex scene," he whispered.

Jack grinned. All their plays were good. The one about the loony king? Jack had seen that one three times. He picked up the wafer. "Sounds flash, Booker John."

"Better not wait," the actor said. "You're not the only one moving on. We'll be off-station in three days. Soon as Perihelion is over."

"So soon?" It seemed like Booker John had always been on Freedom Station. Seemed like he'd always sat there, drinking whiskey and needling Gert.

"We've stayed longer than planned as it is. That little unpleasantness between Pallas and New Oslo pranked our travel arrangements." Booker John spread out his hands. "And much as I love Freedom Station, we have a responsibility to the rest of the system. Perseverance, Beijing II, Independence Station, Seattle Prime, Hubbard. They need a little culture, too." He reached into his pocket and carefully deposited two trade chips on the bar top. "I'll be sure to add Liberty to our itinerary as well."

"That would be cosmic, Booker John," Jack said. And he meant it.

Jack pocketed the chips before the actor was out the door, and just as Gert came bustling around the end of the bar. "Dish up two bowls of chowder and an extra-large order of fried kelp." She started pulling on the synale tap. "And don't take the whole night doing it."

True fact. There were things on Freedom he'd miss. And things he wouldn't miss at all.

Fast Marco, who ran the mining-supply shop on Gagarin, showed up about five minutes before closing. "You ready to go, Gert?"

"In a minute." She had her wafer out, tallying up the day's receipts. Checking Jack's figures. Even though she knew they were right. Jack's figures were always right.

The pub was empty, finally, except for the tinjock. She still hadn't moved from her stool. If her eyes weren't open, Jack would have thought she'd passed out.

Fast Marco leaned in the doorway, chewing a nicotine stick. "Hear you're leaving us, Jack."

Jack looked up from where he was rebooting the vac bot. "True fact." Seemed like news went around the station faster than light came from the sun.

"I got a nice little zip scooter in the shop. Refurbished. Make you a sweet deal."

Two weeks ago—spam, two days ago—Jack would have thought it was a joke. A bad joke. Now he fingered the chips in his pocket. "I might just come by before I leave."

"A pub boy with a zip scooter." Gert stowed her wafer and came around the end of the bar. "Makes about as much sense as a bot with brains." She tilted her head toward the tinjock. "Make sure she's out by closing. We don't want another code violation."

"Hustle it up, Gert," Fast Marco said. "I want to get up to the casino before all the luck runs out."

"No such thing," Jack said, quick, before Gert could. He grinned and shook a finger at Fast Marco. "There's no such thing as luck out here in the Great Maybe."

Gert frowned. "It's a true fact. Only Earthies and loonies rely on luck. All you can trust is your own skill and your own wits."

"And don't you ever forget it," Jack and Fast Marco finished together.

"You know I'm right," Gert said, elbowing past Fast Marco. Thank Calisto, the door closed behind them before Jack could hear the rest of the speech.

He turned back to the vac bot.

"Nice place Gert's got here."

Jack jumped and nearly knocked over the bot.

But it was only the tinjock. It was the first time he'd heard her say anything.

"Real nice place." Her voice was hoarse and raspy, like it didn't get used too much. She was sitting up now, looking around the room. Looking a little surprised to see where she was.

Jack stood up. "Only licensed pub in the Workers' Sector. Food, drink, inhalants, and sprays." He pointed at the shelves behind the bar. "Everything you need to deaden space lag and ease your adjustment. Can I get you something else?" She'd been drinking pretty steadily for the past three hours. He doubted she could get much more adjusted. He glanced at the chron. "It'll have to be your last order."

She tipped her glass and drank down the last swallow of her whiskey. "I'm good," she said. "Real good." She pulled off her yellow stretchy hat and rubbed her bald head. The electrodes, running up and down her scalp, winked and glinted in the lights.

Jack tried not to stare. But, honest to Phobos, tinjocks just looked faulty.

She tapped the electrode closest to her left ear. "The meds gave me a deluxe set. On a good day, I can pick up broadcasts from Alpha Centauri."

"True fact?" Jack said. Like he hadn't heard that one before. Not that many tinjocks were big talkers. "What ship do you jock for?"

She pursed her lips. "You might say I'm a free agent at the moment. You might say I'm waiting for reassignment."

No tinjock waited around for reassignment. Not if the Company wanted to keep the ships flying. But Jack just nodded. She wasn't the first client he'd heard massage the truth.

"Name's Silver," she added. Her amber eyes were bright as go-lights. "I heard you talking about all the Earthies up at the dock. You get many of them here in the pub, Jack?"

"A few. They stop by after they take the tour of the fish and veggie farms." Jack shrugged. "You know, checking out how the workers live. So they can say they did."

She tipped up the glass and sucked in an ice cube. The ice crunched and popped under her teeth. "And I heard you were moving on. Heading out to Liberty."

Seemed like she'd heard an awful lot, sitting there. "That's right," Jack said. "You ever been there?"

"Oh. Sure. Liberty's a good berth." She looked around the pub. "Little more up-to-date then old Freedom, of course. Little more state-of-the-art."

Jack nodded. "Yeah. That's what I heard."

She sucked up another ice cube. "You might want to have a little extra credit stored up, before you go out there. Just as a cushion, you know. Help you get settled in. Help ease your adjustment." Her teeth crunched, her bright eyes watching him.

Jack stared right back. Extra credit? "You selling something?" He glanced toward the door. "You'll have to wait for Gert."

"I'm not selling." Silver glanced toward the door, too. Then she leaned forward, crooking her finger to draw Jack closer. "More like I'm buying," she whispered. "I'm willing to pay, see. I'm willing to pay for someone to do a little spying."

The hairs on the back of his neck tickled, like someone had opened a cold atmo vent right behind him. "You mean, like a spook? Like a Company spook?"

A little smile played across Silver's thin lips and then disappeared. "Well, not so much like a Company spook. Something a little friendlier than that." She checked the door again. "I'm looking for some baggage. Baggage missing from the *Ray Bradbury*."

The *Bradbury* had docked two days before. Barely stayed long enough to refuel. Jack shrugged. "You ask at the baggage office up at the plaza? That's where most lost things end up." The ones that didn't end up in some spacer's locker.

Silver was shaking her head. "I'm not getting the Company involved, kid. I just want to find one particular lost item." She held up her hands in front of her, her fingers cupped and curved. "I'm looking for a maintenance bot."

Jack blinked. "A maintenance bot?" And then he laughed. He couldn't help it. "Holy Titan. I just saw a swarm of them repairing a holo. Go anywhere on the station. You'll run into maintenance bots all over the place."

Silver sighed. Like he was being dim. Like she'd hoped for more. "This one is different. This bot is special."

"Special," Jack repeated. It was like saying one of the floor tiles was special.

"It's smarter than a normal bot. It can work alone. It has extended memory capacity."

"It's been modified?" Jack straightened up. "Modifying bots is against Company regs. Only official Company manufacturers can modify bots."

Silver rubbed at her electrodes. "Which is why this bot is really valuable, kid. Why its memory is valuable. To the right people."

And it was like winning a game of Home Port, when the last disk drops into the bottom slot. What could you store in the extended memory of a little bot? The flight plan of some heavy-loaded freighter. The coordinates to a miner's big strike. Even a sci guy's core analysis of a newfound asteroid.

Lots of people would pay lots of credit to get hold of data like that.

Silver was watching him. Like she knew he was figuring it out, finally getting it. "I heard this pub is the place to come if you've got some"—she paused and the smile flickered and died again—"unusual goods to sell." She glanced down at the cryo can of coffee beans. "If you want to make a certain kind of deal."

True fact, that. Especially since Gert paid the security guards to turn a blind eye. "So why are you talking to me about all this? Why aren't you talking to Gert?"

"Oh, I'm betting a kid like you hears all kinds of stuff

old Gert never gets a whisper of. Here in the pub." Silver nodded toward the door. "All around the station." She leaned forward again. "I'm betting you know more about what's going on than most of the Company admins."

Like he'd stumbled out of Quarantine yesterday. Like he'd fall for that kind of spam. "So what you're saying is, you'll pay me for—" He nearly said "for spying," but he stopped himself. "You'll pay me for any data I pick up."

She held up her hand. "I'll pay you for good data. I'll pay you for data that helps me find this bot."

"How much?"

And now Silver grinned. She dug into the pocket of her blue flight suit and pulled out a little black plexy bag. She tossed it, and Jack caught it in midair. "I'll pay you that right now. Just to seal our deal. You bring me any data about baggage off the *Bradbury*, and I'll pay you three times what you've got in there."

Jack weighed the bag in his hand. Probably ten, maybe twelve, trade chips. Easy. "Where are you staying?"

"I've got a hotel room in the Visitors' Sector." Silver stood and pulled on her hat. "But I'll be around." She held out her hand and, after a second, Jack shook it. Her fingers were as hard and cold as the ice cubes in her glass. She strode out of the pub. Fast and steady. Like she hadn't been drinking anything stronger than water.

Jack opened the bag and spilled the chips out onto the bar. Twelve. And maybe three times more? It would be flash, truly flash, if he could get his own scooter. Take it to Liberty. Show the people.

He knew what Gert would say. *Never count your credit till it's in your account.* And odds were good the tinjock was loony. Loony or lying.

Jack scooped the chips back into the bag. A maintenance bot with augmented memory? He shook his head and laughed. Now that was loony. He slid the bag into his pocket with his tips. Of course, it wouldn't hurt to keep his ears open.

THREE

GERT WAS watching the dailies on the grid wafer when Jack stumbled in from his room the next morning. "Halibut harvest is ready," she said. "I'm going down to the farm to check it out." She keyed the wafer off and pointed at the vac bot, which was sucking at some crumbs under the front couch. "It's still missing spots. You'd better go along behind it with the manual broom."

Jack groaned and rubbed his hands across his face. He'd been hoping to get over to the South Dock. Maybe ask around about the *Bradbury*. "Gert. Do the figures. If you'd buy another vac bot, you'd save credit in the long run."

She grinned. Not a pretty sight, first thing in the morning, before he'd even had a caff pill. "Now, why would I need another bot when I've got a perfectly good apprentice instead?" She was out the door before he could think of an answer.

Jack had barely even started to feel the fizz of the caff pill when the vac bot sputtered, choked, and flopped over sideways.

"Stellar." Clearly it was going to be one of those days.

He was hunched over the bot, trying the third reboot, when the pub door slid open.

"We're drekking closed," he snapped.

"Then you should drekking lock the door."

He whipped around. The rat was standing in the doorway, big as Jupiter. She was carrying a miner's pack.

Jack scrambled to his feet. "Most people believe the sign. They don't just come barging in."

She held up the pack. "I heard you take barter."

"We're *closed*," Jack said. Did she need ear plants or something? "Besides, we don't barter with Earthies." He pointed at the pack. "You stole that. You stole that pack from some poor miner just in from prospecting."

The rat rolled those greeny-green eyes. "Oh, spare me the rant. Like I don't know half the economy of this space station is based on stealing."

It was a true fact. But Jack wasn't going to admit it to her. He leaned back against table four. "I suppose you stole the clothes, too." At least she'd lost the fresh-out-of-Quarantine outfit. And some of the smell. But now she was wearing red farmer coveralls. About two sizes too big. And a pair of the slippers the sci guys wore in the labs. Plus, she'd gotten a yellow tinjock's hat. She looked like a farmer who grew wafers and just happened to navigate ships. "You look like a dink."

She looked down at herself. And then glared back up at him. "Believe me, if I could have found something better, I wouldn't be wearing this." She shook the pack at him. "I was told you take barter. And I've got good stuff."

"I don't barter with rats," Jack said, crossing his arms.

Not, he realized, that any other rat had ever tried before.

She shook the pack again. "Really good stuff."

Jack was watching the pack swing from side to side. "I don't have any spare credit."

"I don't want credit. I want food." And she gave him a little grin. Like she knew she was hooking him. Reeling him in.

It was a really annoying little grin.

The way she was tossing the pack around, you could tell it wasn't very heavy. Probably didn't have any ore chunks or dust bags. But you never knew what might be in a miner's pack. Jack sighed. "Let's see what you've got."

She started to open the top. And then she turned her back. Like a little kid opening Aphelion presents. "Socks," she said over her shoulder.

Jack snorted.

"A pair of inners?"

She glanced back. And Jack knew they were both wondering who goes out hunting ore in the Asteroid Belt with only one pair of inners. She started to smile, and just for a second, Jack nearly did, too.

He shook his head. "Definitely don't want those inners."

She dug back into the pack. And then she turned all the way around. A big grin on her face.

He knew she thought she had something cosmic.

"A vid?" She held it out flat on her hand.

It was like the caff finally fizzed, all along Jack's spine. But he managed to keep his voice bored and bot-flat. "A vid?" he said. He didn't know if she knew the Company had closed the library half an orbit ago. "What's the title?"

She pressed the talky. "*Treasure Island*," the vid said in a deep, male voice. It reminded Jack a little of Booker John.

The rat's grin widened. "Oh. Hey. I know this one. We watched it in school."

Jack couldn't stop himself. "What's it about?"

"It's stellar. It's about pirates—they're like rakers. Only with boats."

"Boats?"

"Ships. But they don't fly. They go on water."

"Water?" Jack laughed. "You mean like in the ponic tanks? Ships in the fish tanks?" He laughed again. "That's cracked. They'd never fit."

"No, no." The rat's fingers closed on the vid. "Look," she said, and Jack could tell she was trying to keep her voice low and calm, "it's in out-of-the-box condition. Hardly ever been viewed. You can barter it yourself, if you don't want to keep it." She glanced behind him at the cook pot, the chowder simmering away, the chop bots working on the onions. "It's at least worth a bowl of soup."

Jack shook his head. "That chowder there. That's the best on the station." He rubbed his forehead. "I'll give you one eel roll," he said finally.

"*Three* rolls. All squirt cheese," she said, fast as light.

"Two rolls. One eel. One cheese."

"Done," she said. And she tossed him the vid.

He slid it into his pocket. And he remembered Silver.

But could tell he had to be careful what he said to this rat. He pointed to the pack. "There's nothing else good, is there? There isn't any tech or anything?"

"What?" Her voice was Earthie-loud, like it was the last thing she'd expected him to say. And then she laughed. "If I had tech to barter, do you think I would have settled for two lousy rolls?"

"Well." He couldn't argue with that. He shrugged. "Never mind." As he went back behind the bar, he added, "And our rolls aren't lousy."

The rat was up on a stool by the time he turned around. She stowed the pack, carefully, between her feet. And she took off the hat.

"Spam," Jack said. Somewhere she'd gotten hold of some red Perihelion beads, and she'd braided them into her hair. But they didn't hang down around her shoulders. The hair and the beads stood straight up. Like glowing red feelers.

She put her hand up to touch them. "What's wrong?"

"Nothing. Nothing at all. Looks cosmic."

"I just thought . . . you know . . ." She dropped her hand and glared at him. "I'm trying to blend in."

"Sure you are. Just keep the hat on." He pulled out two kelp flats. Not the fresh ones Luna had delivered yesterday. The ones from the expired bin.

The rat was checking her reflection in the cook pot. "I walked all the way around the Loop Road yesterday, right through the Visitors' Sector. All the way back around, right out in the open."

"Then obviously your disguise is working." Jack got out the tub of eel paste and the can of squirt cheese and a plexy blade.

"Walking around the loop was boggling, though." The rat shook her head, and the beads rattled. "I just couldn't believe I was really walking around *inside* a giant rock."

Like it would feel normal to walk around on the *outside* of one. Jack uncorked the paste and started spreading it on one of the flats.

"Were you tested for food service?" the rat asked.

"You think I'm poisoning you or something?" He pointed the plexy blade at her.

She frowned. "I was just asking. We hear a lot of rumors back on Earth. About how things are done out here. About how work is assigned."

"Freedom Station isn't the Junkyard. We follow the rules and regs, like everybody else." He finished spreading the paste. "The Company tested me, back in Nursery. I tested in the ninety-fifth percentile for this job."

"Because of all your social skills, I imagine."

Jack shot her a look. But she was just sitting there. All big green eyes and ridiculous hair. He rolled up the flat.

"I'm good with numbers. That's why I was chosen. This job's more than just feeding dinks, you know." He flipped open the second flat.

"I'm sure it is." She leaned forward, watching him uncap

the cheese. "Are you snugging with that girl?"

"What?" Cheese shot out of the can and halfway across the bar.

"That girl you were talking to yesterday in the plaza. The one with the long hair." The rat raised her eyebrows. "Are you snugging with her?"

"No! Yes! Maybe." Jack banged down the can of cheese and more sprayed out. "What do you care?"

"I don't care." The rat frowned. "What do you care if I care?"

"I didn't say I cared if you care." Jack stopped and took a long, deep breath. Carefully he wiped the cheese off his chin. Then he frowned. "You were in the plaza yesterday? You were watching me in the plaza?"

She straightened up, her eyes even wider, greener. "I happened to see you. As I was leaving. I just happened to see you."

"And then you followed me? You followed me here to the pub?"

"Of course I didn't follow you." She blew out a little, exasperated puff. "I was here before you. Remember?"

"But . . ." A headache was starting. Right between his eyes. He picked up the cheese can again and carefully sprayed the flat. He closed it up and shoved both rolls across the bar. "Here. Go. Now. Before Gert gets back."

But the rat just grabbed the cheese roll, her hands trembling a little. She took a big bite and then another. "Is Gert your mother?" she mumbled.

Jack pressed his hand against his forehead. Hard. Where in all the wide solar system did this rat get these ideas? "Of course she's not my mother. Gert's my boss. I told you, the Company assigned me to her pub."

The rat took another bite. "But your parents are here on the station?"

"Are you like a Company researcher or something? You gathering data? You taking the drekking census?"

She shrugged. "I'm just curious. And I haven't had much chance to talk to anybody. People here don't talk much to *rats*." She emphasized the last word and glared at him like this was his fault.

Jack sighed. "My mother went in the composter a long time ago. I was a little kid. I don't really remember her." Although, as soon as he said it, just for a second, he did remember. Short curly black hair. Big brown eyes. Like his own. And a smile. A nice smile. He shook his head. Could've been anybody. Could've been a nanny. "I don't know about my father." He wasn't telling a rat about Liberty. Why bother?

The rat had finished the roll. She licked her fingers, slowly, getting every tiny crumb. "My parents are dead, too," she said.

"Dead?" Nobody ever said "dead," except maybe in vids.

The rat picked up the eel roll and took a bite. "My mom died in the second Northern Hemisphere flu epidemic. I was just a little kid. I don't much remember her." She stared down at the roll and picked off a tiny piece of the flat. "My dad died on the way out here. Contaminants in his sleep bag." She looked up, her face calm, blank. "It happened just after we left Mars. So that was a long time ago, too." She kept looking at Jack, like she was waiting for something.

"They've got a forty-two percent failure rate. Those sleep bags," Jack said finally.

"They never told us that!" The eyes were really big now. Light/dark mod, too. Jack could tell.

He laughed. "They wouldn't tell you, would they? It would ruin the whole relocation program, if you guys decided you didn't want to come out here." He got out the wipe bot and set it to work on the spilled cheese. "After they composted your father, the captain must have dropped you off here." So, technically, she hadn't been dumped. Not by her parents, anyway.

"All Dad's credit went back to the Company. And I didn't have enough to pay for my own passage. They off-loaded me here. They said I had to wait in Quarantine until the next shuttle."

"Wait." Jack held up his hand. "You snuck out of Quarantine?"

She nodded and took another bite of the roll.

"You snuck out of *Quarantine?*" he said again.

"No." She waved her free hand at the room around them. "I'm still in there. This is all a holo vid." She shrugged. "It was easy. They thought I was with this big family heading for Hubbard. I just walked right out."

Nobody ever snuck out of Quarantine.

The rat was looking at him, her head tilted to one side. "My name's Kit, by the way."

"Jack," he said. It was always hard to tell with Earthies, but she had to be close to his age. "What's your apprenticeship?"

"Diplomat corps." And she said it like he was supposed to be impressed. "I don't suppose the Company assigned any diplomats to Freedom Station." She looked around, like maybe they kept one stashed under the back couch.

"Oh, yeah. We had one," Jack said. "Only we put him out the exhaust vent, last cycle."

She was too dim to get the joke. "I have all the qualifications," she said. "When they planned me, my parents bought all the right mods. Intelligence, creativity, social skills, verbal skills, physical agility."

"Physical agility?"

She ignored him and pointed at her hair. "This was on sale. Some kind of package deal with the eyes."

"All the advantages nature didn't provide," Jack said, just like the latest ad on the grid.

"And now I'm stuck here. On this rusty space station." And she finished the roll, chewing it up in fast, sharp bites.

"The Company will be happy to shuttle you back to Earth. You could get right back to diplomat training."

"I can't." She looked up at him, straight and direct. She still had that "I know everything" Earthie look. But she looked angry, too. Angry and determined. And maybe just a little bit sad. All at the same time. "I have to get to Seattle Prime."

"Seattle Prime?" Jack laughed. "You think Freedom's rusty, Seattle Prime is the armpit of the solar system. They don't even have real food on that colony. No ponics. No nothing."

But she still had that look. "I promised," she said. "I promised my father."

Outside, Gert walked past the window.

"Spam!" Jack said.

But Kit was already grabbing up the pack and her hat. By the time the front door slid open, she had disappeared through the rear door, into the back corridor.

Jack started stowing away the eel paste, the plexy blade, the wiper bot. "Hey, Gert," he said.

And he saw that Kit had stolen the can of squirt cheese.

FOUR

THE PUB was packed for the rest of the day. Everybody eager to get the holiday started. The juke bot blared out "Around We Go Again" and "Lost in the Black" on continuous replay.

"It'll be even better tomorrow, Jack," Gert said, wiping sweat out of her blue eye. "What with the parade and the celebration afterward. People will want to get loosened up before the festivities begin."

There was a loud crash. The farmer who had been ring-dancing on table two had fallen off. "They get any looser," Jack said, "they'll be floating halfway to Deneb."

"More synale!" the geeks on the front couch roared.

"Keep your inners on!" Gert roared back.

During the midafternoon lull, Jack dug out the grid wafer, keyed it on, and checked the dailies. Rats usually got scooped in their first two minutes on the station. But there were no reports of any rats being impounded.

Drek. He knew he ought to report the use of station resources by a noncontributing inhabitant. Jack keyed off the wafer. He remembered the green eyes and that fierce, intense look. Of course, Freedom Station's atmo consumption wasn't really his problem anymore. In forty-four days, he'd be on the *Isaac Asimov* heading out to Liberty.

What could be so important on Seattle Prime?

An hour before closing, two geeks came in and took the back couch in the corner. They ordered one small mug of synale. To share.

Gert frowned. "Might as well have stayed back in their lab."

But the docker who joined them about half an hour later ordered tall mugs for all of them.

When Jack carried the drinks over, the geeks were leaning forward, listening to the docker. "Wouldn't usually trust a junkie, but I know this one personally. She's got the goods out there. Bot parts and state-of-the-art components. All unclaimed baggage from the *Bradbury*."

It took Jack a second to process what she was saying. And another second to realize all three of them were staring up at him, like they thought he was a Company spook. "You got a problem, kid?" one of the geeks asked.

"No. No problem." Jack slid the mugs onto the table and carried the empty tray back to the bar.

He slid the tray onto the bar. The docker and the geeks were huddled even closer together. Between the rat and the Perihelion crowds, he'd just about forgotten about Silver.

It was almost like he could feel her cold fingers. But he thought about the plexy bag in his locker back in his room. He thought about the trade chips inside. True fact. Thirty-six more chips would definitely help ease his adjustment to Liberty.

"Snap out of it." Gert poked him with her long finger, the one she'd had transplanted after the grinder accident.

"You standing around dreaming about zip scooters?"

Jack laughed. "That's exactly what I'm dreaming about, Gert." And he laughed even harder at the look on her face.

It took forever for the chron to flip around to closing time. And even longer for Gert to get everything prepared for the next day. "So we're ready for the rush tomorrow," she said, checking the synale kegs for the third time.

Jack waited until she finally muttered her way upstairs. Waited until he heard her door slam and her chair creak. Waited until he heard the low whine of her vid player warming up.

And then he was out the door.

It was full night. The overheads weren't even glowing. All the streets in the Workers' Sector were empty. The only sound was the faint squeak of the floor tiles under his feet. He was jogging by the time he reached the Loop Road and made the turn.

The building lights in the Visitors' Sector were on full bright. And the streets were noisy and crowded. Mostly with Earthies, eager for distraction. So they didn't have too much time to think about where they were going after they left Freedom.

Not that they could exactly change their minds now.

Jack started with the obvious places, the places that fit with a tinjock's credit. The smaller hotels, the cheaper restaurants. And he asked around. Sean waiting tables at Ishmael's; Amalthea running Slap Happy at the casino. They hadn't seen any tinjocks.

There was a crowd trying to get into the gym. Rigel was running credit checks at the door. Jack pushed his way to the front of the line. "Hey, Rige. You checked any tinjocks in lately?"

Rigel shook his head. "I wish. Be better than this bunch." He let three more Earthies through the door and nodded to a group clustered around the nearest treadmill. "You gotta watch them every minute, honest to Phobos." One of the Earthies started shaking the towel bot. Rigel moved toward him, then stopped. "By the way, you heard anything more about Annie's party?"

"Not yet," Jack said.

"Should be stellar, though. Knowing Annie." Rigel turned toward the Earthie. "Hey! Spam-for-brains!"

Jack pushed his way back out onto the sidewalk.

He looked up and down the street. No sense checking the swank hotel, reserved for the Company admins. Or the private colony clubs. All the Beijing II people in one building. The Quito Revisited people in another.

An Earthie bumped into him, knocking him against the wall. "Watch where you're going, stinking spacer," she muttered.

"I hope your sleep bag fouls—" And then Jack saw Silver.

She was in front of the Pallas club, just stepping off the sidewalk. Jack watched her bright yellow hat, bobbing through the crowd as she crossed the street and disappeared into one of the public meeting halls.

Jack dashed after her. The door to the hall was already shut. The credit box on the wall said, "Admission required."

Jack pressed his finger to the DNA reader and slipped inside as soon as the door opened.

After the overbright lights outside, the darkness was a shock. Jack had to stop to let his eyes adjust.

Circular rows of seats spiraled around a small stage, all of them full. Mostly Earthies. All of them, thank Calisto, completely silent. All of them sitting forward, watching the stage intently.

Three really dysfunctional-looking women were clustered around a big cook pot. And then Booker John walked on.

"Macbeth," Jack said.

The Earthie in the seat in front of him jerked around and hissed, "Shh!"

"Sorry," Jack hissed back.

It was always something to see, how different Booker John looked when he was working. It wasn't just the funny clothes. Or the wig and the makeup. It was something completely different about Booker John himself. Tonight, standing up there on the stage, he looked younger, smaller, meaner.

And then Jack spotted Silver leaning against the back wall, chewing on a nicotine stick. She was watching Booker John, too.

Jack made his way over to her, ignoring the curses of the audience. He was careful to whisper this time. "I've got some data."

Silver jumped. Like he'd tapped her with a stun rod. People seated nearby turned their heads and glared. Silver grabbed Jack's arm and pulled him toward the exit.

There was a loud boom, like a rain-warning from the weather cycle. The whole audience gasped, and an enormous head rose out of the cook pot on the stage.

"Holy—" Jack slowed down to watch, but Silver kept dragging him behind her.

Outside, she flicked the nicotine stick into the street. "What did you hear? You got the bot?"

Jack tried to pull his arm loose, but her grip was too tight. "A docker was in the pub tonight. She was talking to some geeks about components and tech gear. In unclaimed baggage from the *Bradbury*."

Silver's fingernails dug into his arm. "Who's got this baggage? Where?"

"The docker said they'd have to deal with a junkie." Jack narrowed his eyes, watching her closely. "So it must be out in the Junkyard."

"The Junkyard?" Silver said, her raspy voice sinking a little.

"Right. The station maintains a parts depot out behind the Shipyard," Jack said helpfully. "They've got just about one of every kind of ship welded together out there. Obsolete freighters, transports, skiffs, runners. You name it."

Silver shook his arm, hard enough to wrench his shoulder. "I know all about the Junkyard, kid."

Jack grinned. It was good to know even Silver would think twice about going out there. About dealing with the junkies who lived out there. It made her seem just a little more human.

Silver let go of Jack, and one finger eased up under the edge of her hat. Scratched. "You sure this data is good, kid? You're not jerking me around? Having a little spacer fun?"

Jack took his time, straightening up his coverall, dusting himself off. *Spacer fun.* "I'm just telling you what I heard. The docker didn't specifically mention a maintenance—"

Silver grabbed him again and jerked him back against the wall, into the shadows. "Not so loud." She looked up and down the street. And relaxed, slowly. She let go of Jack and tried for a smile. "You're right, kid. You did just what I asked. You did good." She pulled out a chip and handed it over.

"Hey!" Jack held it up. "You said three times as many."

Silver leaned in, just a little, her weight pressing him back against the wall. "I wasn't implanted yesterday, kid. If this data's good, you'll get paid the rest. Call that a down payment." She flicked his collar. "Trust me."

She turned and disappeared into the crowd.

Trust her? Drekking tinjock. Jack nearly tossed the trade chip out into the street. Gert was right. You couldn't trust anybody out in the Black.

But his data was good. He knew it was. What were the odds of this being some other piece of lost baggage from the *Bradbury*? It had to be the stuff Silver was looking for. And as soon as she came back from the Junkyard, he'd be right there behind her. Right there to get his share of the deal.

Drekking tinjock. He slid the chip into his pocket.

A shout rang out from the hall behind him. He'd already

paid to go in. No sense wasting the credit. At least he could still watch the end of the play.

Two women and a man were standing on the stage. One of the women was pulling at her hands. "Out, damned spot! Out, I say!" She sounded really sad. Really upset. Like she'd gotten a bad limb transplant, and she couldn't afford to sue the med.

Jack settled into Silver's spot on the back wall just as Booker John came out, shouting something about cloning.

When the play was over, and the applause had finally died down, Jack followed the crowd back out onto the street. He stood for a minute, blinking in the light. Everything looked just a little flatter, a little faker. Even for the Visitors' Sector.

Booker John came around the back of the building. He was out of his costume already, back in his faded and patched coverall, his brown hair pulled back in a braid again. Back to being Booker John. "Jack! I saw you come in. Did you like it?"

"Oh, it was flash. True fact. One of your best."

"The fight at the end?" Booker John thrust his hand forward, like he was holding a big laser blade.

"Stellar." Jack grinned. And then he frowned. "But sort of sad, too."

The audience was still filing out past them. None of them even looked at the actor twice.

"I saw your friend leave early," Booker John said. "Guess she's not a fan of Shakespeare."

"My friend? Oh." Silver. Jack shook his head. "She's not a friend. She's just a loony tinjock. Got a glitchy electrode, maybe."

Booker John raised his eyebrows.

Jack grinned. He knew how Booker John loved a good story. But he lowered his voice. "She's looking for a modified maintenance bot. Equipped with memory enhancements. She's got the buyers all lined up, I guess."

"She's got buyers for a maintenance bot?" Booker John looked around, and sure enough, there was a swarm, repairing the DNA reader outside Ishmael's.

"She's going out to the Junkyard to find this bot," Jack said. "She's going to do a deal with a junkie."

"With a junkie?"

"With a junkie," Jack said.

"To find a modified bot." Booker John said it slowly and carefully, like it was a line he was going to have to remember later. He shook his head, smiling. "The risks people will take just to earn a little more credit. It's inspiring."

There was a shout over by the arcade. More voices answered. Getting louder. People started pushing. Some trying to get closer, some moving away. The crowd parted, and Jack saw two groups of Earthies—Perseverance and Hubbard, by their patches—facing each other in the street.

"Ah. Just like the Montagues and the Capulets." Booker John was grinning. "I do love the way Earthies drag everything out here with them. They just have to have their old grudges and hatreds to keep them warm."

Guard platforms shrieked, coming in over the rooftops. Immediately the crowd ringing the colonists started dispersing.

"I gotta go," Jack said. Gert would vent if he got picked up in a guard roundup.

"Time for us all to go," Booker John said. "Thanks for coming tonight, Jack," he added. And he melted away into the crowd.

Jack stepped back closer to the wall and started walking, slowly. Innocently.

The guards were off their platforms, their stun rods out, pushing toward the two groups of Earthies. "Stay calm!" one of them shouted. "Nobody move," the other one added.

The people in front of Jack wavered. He started to walk faster.

And he caught a glimpse of something white, wiggling through the crush.

But when he looked again, the rat was gone.

FIVE

THE NEXT morning Gert spun the grid wafer across the bar to Jack. "Bounce for you. Listen to it quick." Like he got thirty or forty every day.

Jack keyed up the volume. Annie's vocal came out of the wafer, her voice high and happy. "Personal message for Jack," she said. "Party, party, party. 1900 hours today. North Dock plaza. Just us spacers." There was a little echo, a glitch, like the bounce had caught. "Oh," Annie said. "Bring your own goodies. Be there or be flattened in the eternal vacuum of space!" And her laugh echoed in the empty pub.

He listened to it once again. Mostly because Gert was still standing there. And just to hear Annie laugh.

This would be his last Perihelion. His last Perihelion on Freedom Station.

He looked up at Gert. Both the green eye and the blue eye were glinting at him. He slid the wafer back to her. "What?"

She pointed to the shelves. "Start setting out glasses. We're gonna be busy."

The door slid open. "Welcome back the sun!" the first customers shouted.

"Oh, spam," Jack muttered.

Busy didn't even begin to describe it. By the time Gert

shouted that they were closing, even though it was earlier than usual, Jack's legs felt like he'd run all the way to Pluto and back. Twice.

Gert was shoving out the last customers, two sci guys, still arguing about alternatives to helium-3. "Give them a light year, and they'll take a parsec." Gert wiped her face with her sleeve. Her hair was sticking up in clumps. "Come on. Let's get this place cleaned up."

"You're helping?" Jack tried to keep the shock out of his voice. But he couldn't.

She started clearing table six. "I heard the vocal. I was young once, too, you know."

Jack shuddered. That was way more than he wanted to think about. But he wasn't going to turn down the help. He glanced at the chron. 1913. Party had already started.

As he put away the last clean glass, Gert held out a sling bag. Something inside clanked and clinked. Jack groaned. "Gert. I'm not making any special deliveries tonight."

"Take it," she said. "It's not a delivery. It's for your party."

Jack took it and looked inside. Four boxes of pixie dust, some vials of glitter, a bag of zyggy, two bottles of crème de menthe. "Cosmic." He looked up at her. "For the party? True fact?"

"About to expire anyway, most of it." Gert scratched at something above her ear, like she had an especially nasty itch there. "You did good work. Today." She coughed once. Then again. "You're a good apprentice, Jack. Anybody'd be lucky to have you."

He blinked. It was almost like walking into Booker John's play the night before. Only this made even less sense.

Gert's eyes narrowed. "Of course—"

"There's no luck in the Great Maybe," he finished. He put the strap of the bag over his shoulder. "Thanks, Gert."

She poked him in the chest with that long, hard finger. "Remember, you got a regular working day tomorrow. We'll have the post-Perihelion cleanup."

Jack nodded. "Right." He watched her pull on her jacket. "You gonna be in the parade, Gert? Or just dancing in the streets?"

"Perihelion, spamihelion." She smoothed down her hair. "Station's orbit doesn't matter to me. I've got a spot reserved up at the casino. Don't expect to see me before tomorrow morning." She stopped in the pub's door and looked back. "And remember. Don't do anything I wouldn't do, Jack." He could still hear her cackling halfway down the alley.

Ollie and Io and three of Io's workers went past, all dressed as the rings of Saturn. "Welcome back the sun!" Ollie shouted.

Jack grinned. "Welcome back the sun!" he shouted back.

The Loop Road was already blocked by the parade when he got there. Annie's parents went by, dressed as solar flares. They were followed by some farmers, all wearing radiation shields. Fast Marco marched by in the techno troop, all of them juggling scrub bots. Fast Marco waved to Jack without dropping a bot.

Last Perihelion, just before they'd been assigned their apprenticeships, Jack and Rigel and Annie had been chosen to roll the big model sun around the station. Only they'd gone too fast, and it had gotten away from them, up in the Visitors' Sector. They'd barely managed to stop it before it rolled right through the window at Ishmael's. Jack laughed, remembering it, remembering the look on Rigel's face when he'd thought they were all compost.

Earthies were lined up along the Loop. Watching the parade. Shaking their heads like they'd never seen anything quite like this.

"Jack!" Amalthea and Rigel and Sean were working their way down the sidewalk, bumping through the Earthies. Sean shoved one into the path of the veggie growers' float.

Amalthea was covered, head to toe, in bright blue Perihelion beads. They glowed warmly against her black skin. She grabbed Jack's arm. "You coming to the party?"

He held up the sling bag. "Of course."

Sean was glaring back at the Earthies. "They're so dim. They don't even know what we're celebrating."

"Do they have Perihelion?" Jack asked. And he realized he'd never really thought about it.

"What?" Amalthea said.

"On Earth. Do they even have Perihelion?"

"Who cares what they do on Earth?" Rigel said. "I'm going to a party right here on Freedom."

They had to work their way through the parade, dodging

the troop of Nursery kids, all wearing big sun hats and singing the station anthem. But on the other side of the Loop, they caught a tram, right away, heading for the North Dock.

A little family of Earthies—mother, father, two little girls—was clustered around the map holo. They shifted to one side as Jack and the others climbed into the trailer. Sean made a face at them, and one of the little girls hid behind her mother.

But the other kid glared up at them, her eyes big and bright blue.

And Jack thought about telling her to be careful. He thought about warning her not to get dumped. But Amalthea and Rigel pushed him toward the back of the trailer.

The North Dock plaza was empty. Except for Annie. She was standing in front of the Armstrong holo, almost like she was talking to the old guy. She was draped in Perihelion beads, too. They hung in long strands, past her shoulders, down to her waist, glowing green and red and blue. Her coverall was bright green and tight as a pair of inners.

As he got closer, Jack realized it was a pair of inners.

"We're here!" Rigel shouted, spreading his arms wide. "You can start the party!"

"Thank Calisto!" Annie reached out and took Jack's hand. "And the party started a long time ago."

Jack looked around the empty plaza. "Where?"

Annie pointed up the station's high rock wall. "Eli got us the codes to a warehouse room. Up on the docking and arrivals level. We have the whole place to ourselves."

"Stellar!" Amalthea said.

"Welcome back the sun!" Sean shouted.

"You mean up in zero gee?" Jack said.

Here on the floor, the station had full grav. But at its center, there was no gravity at all. Jack could do all the equations that explained it. He could compute the mass and the rate of spin. And he knew zero grav made it possible for the ships and shuttles to dock with the station.

But understanding it didn't mean he liked it.

The rest of them were laughing. "You'll need to get used to it, Jack," Annie said. "For the trip out to Liberty."

True fact. Jack let her drag him over to the right lift and watched as she entered the code.

The lift started as soon as they were all inside. As they rose up the station's wall, Jack could feel the grav disappearing. Like he was losing weight. Losing something inside of himself. His hands, feet, hair, stomach all lightened, rose up. And he was floating. He would have grabbed the sissy bar except Annie was holding his hand. He swallowed, but his stomach kept right on heading up toward his throat.

"Just keep breathing, Jack," Annie said. And she squeezed his hand.

Amalthea and Rigel were laughing like Earthies, like they'd never been in zero gee before in their entire lives. And Sean—who had always been a big showoff, ever since Nursery—Sean was turning big, lazy somersaults in the middle of the lift.

"Main docking level," the lift said, and the doors slid open.

If they went right, they'd come to the shuttle docking port and the arrivals terminal, all unlit and quiet today. "This way, this way." Annie swam out, towing Jack behind her, and turned left. They coasted past two closed doors and then an open one. Jack glanced inside the warehouse room; it was pitch-dark, empty, and cavernous. The big storage spaces always kind of gave him the creeps. Built out onto the outside of the station. Not really a part of the station at all.

Annie stopped in front of the next door, which was closed up tight.

Jack could hear the throb of the music.

Annie keyed the panel, and the door opened. "This is it!" she yelled at the top of her lungs.

A couple dozen portable juke bots, meshed together, were pulsing out the same song. Not, Jack was glad to hear, "Around We Go Again" or "Lost in the Black." Something punkno-swing.

Rigel and Sean and Amalthea were already swimming into the room.

Jack hung, for a minute, clinging to the edge of the doorway.

Kids floated everywhere. He tried to do a quick count but gave up in the dim light. It looked like Annie had invited everybody out of Nursery but not old enough to earn full wage.

Annie let go of his hand. "Welcome back the sun!" she

shouted. She pushed off and soared over to Amalthea, who had started dancing, spinning around and around, head over heels, her blue beads flowing out around her like comet tails. Annie grabbed her hand and started spinning with her.

The lift doors opened again, and three kids—dockers Jack barely knew—swam out. They jostled past, knocking Jack loose from the doorway and shoving him out into the room. He flailed, trying to stop, which just made him go faster. He banged against the side wall, ricocheted off, tried to tread air, and smacked into two guys sharing a small cone of fury. They were blipping so hard, they didn't even notice. Jack bounced off them and, by chance, managed to end up at the back wall.

He grabbed a safety strap. Immediately his feet started drifting back and up, twisting him around. He swallowed, trying to keep his stomach somewhere in the middle of his body. The sling bag floated out from his side, like an extra arm. He grabbed it and pulled it closer to him.

Most kids were dancing, like Amalthea and Annie, alone or in couples or triplets. Luna and some service workers were sharing fish fries near the hatch to the air lock. Leo and Sayid and a bunch of other kids were playing catch with a sweep bot.

Nova glided over and hovered in front of Jack. She was covered in bright white beads. "Jack, Jack. Guess what I am."

"Got me."

"Super Nova!" she shouted. She spread out her arms and cartwheeled away, laughing hysterically, white light flashing out from her.

And Jack remembered the flash of white the night before. Where was the rat now? Was Kit hiding somewhere, safe and out of the way? Or was she wandering the station, blending in? And was she all alone on Perihelion?

Not even an Earthie should be all alone on Perihelion.

Leo sailed past and hit the wall. He bounced off and grabbed the strap next to Jack. "Jack!" He turned his head, and the beads braided into his hair swirled. "How come you're upside down?"

"There is no upside down in zero gee," Jack said automatically. It was the one thing he remembered from all those mandatory movement classes, back in Nursery. But now that Leo had said it, he realized he was upside down. Or, at least, he *felt* upside down.

Leo pulled himself around so he could face Jack. "So what you're saying is orientation is all relative. What you're saying, in fact, is that everything is relative."

"No. I'm saying I don't think I'm upside down."

Leo's eyes were wide, all big black pupils. He grabbed Jack's sleeve. "Think about it. If there is no up or down, then there is no up or down!" He leaned in closer, and warm synale breath flooded over Jack. "So we can't know if we're up or down!"

Jack patted Leo's arm. "You're thinking way too much

here. It's not good for you. You might hurt yourself. You should go back and play catch."

"No, no, no." Leo tried to drape an arm around Jack's shoulders and missed. "I want to talk to you, Jack. I hardly ever talk to you, and it's important that I talk to you."

Nguyen swam over. Her beads were all red, and she had them around her neck, her waist, her wrists and ankles. They were pulsing in some kind of pattern, like they were sending a bounce. They probably were. She grabbed Leo to stop herself, which pushed both of them into Jack. They all bobbled for a minute. Leo and Nguyen both spun.

"Ha!" Leo said. "Now I'm upside down."

"There is no up or down—" Nguyen started.

"Don't say it." Jack held up his free hand. "Trust me. Don't say it." He wiggled the sling bag off his shoulder. "Look what I brought. Glitter. Pixie dust."

"Jack! You are a hero!" Leo shouted.

Nguyen's eyebrows were arched. "How'd you afford all this? You hack into the DNA bank or something?"

"It's a long story. You wouldn't believe it." Jack handed her the bag. "Here. There's some crème de menthe in there, too."

"Jack." Nguyen's smile gleamed. "I think I love you."

"I think so, too," Leo said. "Jack, I think I love you, too."

"Gather round, kiddies!" Nguyen shouted, just like the nannies used to do. "Time to play Vacuum of Space."

There were shouts and shrieks, and immediately a

cloud of kids surrounded them. Nguyen uncorked the bottle, letting the fat green globules loose.

"No hands!" Leo shouted. "No hands!" Kids started chasing the wobbly bubbles, hands behind their backs, mouths wide open.

A blob smacked against Jack's mouth, and he sucked it in. Sticky and sweet. Tasted just like Perihelion. And he wondered what Perihelion would be like on Liberty.

Annie swam up and took his free hand. "Let's go back down to the plaza!" she shouted.

Her hand was a little sweaty. "I'm good!" Jack shouted back. He looked around the room. "I can do this all night."

Annie laughed and shook her head, all her beads swinging and clicking. "I need a break," she said. "Keep me company."

She pushed off. Jack let go of the strap, and guided by her, they glided across the room and back out to the lift.

As it started down, Jack could feel everything pulling into place, settling comfortably inside of him. So that, by the time they reached the station floor, he felt like he'd come back together. The lift doors opened.

He stumbled a little, getting out.

This end of the station was cool and quiet. The overheads were darkening to early evening.

Annie spread out her arms and turned in a big slow circle. "Feels good. Not so stuffy." She stopped turning and looked at him. "You always have been a grav monkey, Jack," she said. But not like he was pranked. Not like it was faulty.

Jack grinned at her. "I am getting better. I really was just about to let go of that strap."

"Oh. I could see that," Annie said, grinning back. "We'll go up in a minute, and you can show me. We'll dance."

"Dance." Jack nodded. "Sounds stellar."

"Hey! Hey! You guys!" Eli came running across the plaza, with Tranh right behind him. They were both laughing.

Annie put her hands on her hips. "You are so late. Where have you been?"

Eli caught his breath. "We've got it cornered."

"Behind the looky-look booths," Tranh added.

"What?" Annie glanced back at Jack. She was starting to laugh, too. "What have you got cornered?"

They shouted it together. "A rat!"

SIX

FOR A second, everything inside Jack jolted loose. Like he was back in zero gee. "A rat? What rat?"

"A creepy girl." Tranh waved a hand above his head. "Scummy-looking hair."

"Who cares what rat?" Eli nudged Annie. "When was the last time you went on a rat hunt?"

"Remember the one we dunked in the ponic tank?" Tranh said. "In with the kelp?"

"Or the one we trapped over by the composter?" Annie said. "And we told it we were going to put it inside." She looked at Jack. "Remember?"

And he did remember. But those rats had been different. Those rats had been . . . rats. "But—"

"Micah can't keep it trapped behind the booths forever," Eli said.

"Rat hunt!" Tranh started the chant.

"Rat hunt!" Eli joined in. They both started heading back across the plaza. "Rat hunt!"

Annie started after them. "Come on, Jack. This'll be fun. Just like old times."

"Right." Old times.

He followed them across the plaza and down the street. Off in the distance, he could hear the faint beat of the music, the rumble of people still partying. Up ahead, Annie was chanting, too. "Rat hunt! Rat hunt!"

They were walking fast, already past the offices and the guard headquarters, jogging a little past the agents' quarters and into the Commercial Sector. Only two blocks from the booths.

Jack hustled to catch up. "Hey. Wait." They stopped under the lights of Gustav's refit shop. "I've got an idea." Jack pointed down the side alley. "I'll go around in back of the booths. You know, through Fast Marco's yard. In case she goes over the fence."

"Oh. Cosmic idea." Annie's eyes were sparking, as bright as her beads.

Before she could say anything else, Jack turned and started to run down the alley.

The light was on over Fast Marco's door, and the sign said, "Going out of business. Make you a sweet deal." But it always said that. Jack slipped through the gate into the recycler yard.

It was darker here, away from the light. But every kid on Freedom knew the looky-look booths were on the other side of this fence. And every kid on Freedom knew which panel was loose. If you wanted a free seat for the porn vids.

"Here rat, rat, rat."

Jack swore softly. It was Eli, already over on the other side. Close to the entrance to the booths.

And Micah had to be around somewhere. Maybe right on the other side of the fence.

"Kit?" Jack whispered. He pried up the panel.

"Jack?" She came wiggling out. The knees of her coveralls were torn and stained. The hat and the beads were gone. She didn't have the miner's pack, but she did have the little duffel over her shoulder again.

"Rat!" Micah shouted. Close.

"They're chasing me," Kit hissed. "They've been chasing me for half an hour!"

"Where are you, rat?" Micah was right on the other side of the fence. "Hey!" Something clanged. "Hey! Where'd she go?"

The panel rattled.

Jack grabbed Kit's hand. "This way."

"Jack! You got her, Jack?" Annie yelled.

Kit pulled back, staring at him, her eyes flashing green in the low light.

"Go around," Eli shouted. "We've got to go around!" Feet pounded.

"It's not . . . I'm not . . . I'm helping you, for Pluto's sake." Jack gave her a shove toward the gate. "Run!"

And she did run, the bag thumping against her side. Jack hesitated. He'd gone to this much trouble. He couldn't just let them catch her halfway up the street. He ran after her.

She stopped at the corner, looking wildly up and down. Jack pulled her into the gap between the taqueria and the assay office.

The street on the other side was empty. But Jack could hear muffled shouts coming closer.

The weather cycle boomed out a warning, a crack of thunder louder than the one in Booker John's play. "Spam," Jack said. And it started to rain. Cold and hard.

Kit wiped at her face. "It has to rain now?"

"It always rains on Perihelion." Jack glanced behind them. The street was still empty. And then he knew where they could go. He grabbed her hand. "Come on. This way."

They were both soaked by the time they got to the chapel garden.

Jack pushed the gate open. "Come on. They won't look for us in here." True fact. Eli and Annie never visited the chapel.

Kit stopped just inside the gate. "Are these bushes?" She looked down at her feet. "And dirt?"

"It's a garden. It's supposed to be . . ." Jack sighed. "Some old story. I don't know. Some old Earth story about some big garden?" Kit was shaking her head. "Never mind. It's not important."

The path was bordered by lights set into the tiles. They lit the floor, but not much above knee height. With the over-heads almost dimmed to night, they had to watch where they walked. Just as they passed the crouching shadow of the tree stump, he heard the shout. Eli. In the street still, but right outside the gate. Jack pushed Kit behind a clump of bushes, thick with scratchy, prickly leaves. And then he knelt down next to her, so close he could feel her shivering.

For a second, the only sound was the rain.

Then Eli said, loud, "I know they came down here. I saw them."

"Jack! Give us back our rat!" Tranh shouted.

It was very, very quiet again. Just the rain and the tiny rasp of Kit's breathing. Water dripped off the leaves, down Jack's neck.

Footsteps squelched. "You in here, Jack?" Annie said. She sounded uncertain. But she was inside the garden. She was on the path.

"You space-happy, Jack?" It was Micah. He giggled. "You snugging with rats now, Jack?"

"Oh, come on," Eli said. "Even Jack wouldn't snug with an Earthie." And he laughed.

Jack felt Kit's arm jerk. He stared down at his right knee sinking into the mud.

"I'll bet Jack's not even in here," Annie said. Her voice was sharp. Eli and Micah stopped laughing. "I bet he went back to the party."

"I saw—" Eli started.

"This is toxic," Annie said, louder, firmer. "I'm wet, and I'm cold, and I'm going back."

Jack heaved a little sigh. When she talked like that, nobody argued with Annie. Sure enough, the footsteps moved off, out the gate, down the path.

The sound had barely faded when Kit was up and pushing her way out of the bushes. Jack thought she was going to head for the gate, and he was opening his mouth to tell her to wait, to warn her it might be a trick. But she walked, fast, in the opposite direction.

Jack crawled out from under the bush. The rat's shoulders were stiff and straight. Her white hair stuck up like a scrub bot's brushes. She disappeared around a bend in the path.

He looked back at the gate, remembering Micah's giggles. Eli's honking laugh. The tone of Annie's voice. Jack sighed. He'd give them a little while to cool off. Fifteen minutes. Let them get back to the party. Get a little juiced. Get a little more relaxed. Maybe he'd give them half an hour.

He turned and followed the rat down the path.

She was standing in front of the chapel.

"Welcome, visitors of all faiths," the chapel said.

Soft lights lit the low little building and its peeling white paint. A few soggy, skinny bushes crouched on each side of the door. They were almost compost. A few shriveled leaves twitched in the rain.

"This station bogs," Kit said. "The people on this station bog. Cosmically."

"They weren't going to hurt you," Jack said. "It was just a game."

She swung around. "A game? They were going to put me in a ponic tank with the lid closed. They said so. That's not how you treat people!"

"But you're—"

"A rat? I told you, I'm not a rat!"

He'd meant to say "But you're an Earthie." He wiped his

sleeve across his face and nodded toward the chapel door. "We've got ten minutes of rain left. At least. We should go in where it's dry." He stepped forward.

"Welcome, visitors of all faiths," the chapel said again.

"Is the chapel occupied?" Jack asked it.

The program was old and glitchy, not high on anyone's maintenance list. The response took a full half minute. "No one is currently inside," the chapel said. "And the Perihelion service originally scheduled for 2300 hours has been cancelled."

The door swung open, and a light clicked on. Jack went in. Kit was still standing on the path, her hands on her hips. "You coming or not?" Jack asked.

"What if there's some other loony person in there? Somebody who's going to chase me around and try to drown me?"

"There's only me in here. And you're going to drown for sure if you stay out there."

She shook her head, and water flicked across her face. But, finally, she walked in. The door shut behind her.

"This is the chapel?" She turned around. There was barely room for her to do it. "Okay. I didn't think it was possible, but the inside is even worse than the outside."

The whole room shuddered and lurched.

"Hey!" Kit staggered and grabbed Jack's arm. And let it go, quick.

She smelled of wet fabric and Earth. "It's a lift," Jack said. "The actual chapel is Down Below."

They jolted to a stop, and the door slid open. The light in the lift went out. Everything, the lift, the room in front of them, was completely dark.

"What's happening?" Kit's voice was even louder than usual.

"How do you wish to worship?" The chapel's voice was low.

Jack smiled. "Remove the covering."

There was no sound. But, centimeter by centimeter, the floor of the chapel started to glow.

Jack walked out onto the floor. He turned and looked back. Kit was still inside the lift, her white hair and her pale face floating in the darkness.

He opened his hands toward the pinpricks of light blossoming at his feet. "Come stand on the stars."

Kit still didn't move.

"It's okay." He jumped up and down. "It's reinforced plexy."

She eased out of the lift, sliding her feet along. "Holy spam." She was whispering. She stopped sliding, knelt down, and came the rest of the way on her hands and knees. "Holy spam," she said again.

Jack laughed.

"Doesn't it make you dizzy?" Her voice was still low and hushed.

Zero gee made him dizzy. Not this. "You get used to it." He looked down at the stars, coming in from the right, passing underneath them, and disappearing off to the left. He pointed. "There's Vega in Lyra." Kit sat up a little, to see better. "And over there, that fuzzy smudge, that's M13 in the keystone of Hercules."

They both followed the galaxy's flight beneath them until it disappeared.

"Where's Earth?" Kit asked.

"Earth's way too small." He stopped. "And it's hidden by the sun's glare. At Perihelion, things get a little distorted."

Kit sat up straighter and looked around at the rest of the chapel. "Is it always like this? Just the stars in the dark?"

"No. Most people keep the covering rolled out." Jack nodded toward the table on the little stage at one end of the room, a big bowl of water beside it. "Some of them use that stuff. And some of them just sit and watch holos. The walls are all projectos."

Kit looked down at the stars again. "They're going so fast." She reached out a hand, like she was trying to touch one of them, slow it down.

Jack sat down next to her and crossed his legs. Like in Nursery. *Crisscross, I'm the boss.* "The station's moving that fast." He rotated his index finger, like the movement of the station. "One spin every seven minutes. To create gravity."

"You just don't think about it." Her voice was still soft. Not her teaching-vid voice at all. "Until you see it." She leaned forward and pressed both hands flat on the plexy. "And it's so big. You don't think about that, either. How big it all is out there. How far away everything is."

Jack laughed, he couldn't help it. It was such an Earthie thing to say. "It's the Black. Of course it's big. It goes on forever." He pointed again. "There's the Teapot in Sagittarius."

Kit was looking at him, her eyes very dark. The green almost gone. The way a cat's eyes adjust to the dark. "You come here a lot? I didn't think . . ." She shrugged and almost looked embarrassed. "They told us spacers aren't very religious."

"I like to look at it." He ran his hand over the plexy. It was smooth and cold. Almost like he could feel the iciness of the Black right through it. "When I was little—" He stopped. He'd never told anybody this. Not Nguyen. Not Rigel. Not Annie. He took a breath. "When I was little, I'd sit here and pretend this was my ship. You know, that I was flying it through the Black. I'd even compute the trajectories for minimum fuel consumption." He laughed. Quick. Before she could.

But she didn't laugh. "Back on Earth," she said, "my dad used to take me up on the roof of our apartment building at night, and we'd try to see the stars." Her shoulders rose, fell. "You can't see much through the dome and all the exterior pollution. There was never anything like this."

They were both quiet, watching the stars slip away below them, big and little, bright and dim, a river of light.

Kit tilted her head, and Jack knew she was looking at him again. "Do you believe in God, Jack?"

"What?"

"Do you believe something's out there? Something, you know, watching over us?"

"There's nothing out there. That's why they call it the vacuum of space." He laughed. But she didn't. She just sat there, her head tilted, looking at him. Waiting for him. He shrugged. "Sometimes Gert calls it the Great Maybe. She's always saying there's no luck in the Great Maybe."

"Oh," Kit said. "Oh. I like that."

"You like that there's no luck out here?"

"No, dim spacer." And now she was smiling. "The *maybe* part. Do you think she means 'maybe' or 'may be'?" She separated the two words out, slow and careful.

"What difference does it make?"

"It makes all the difference." Kit reached out and rested her hand on his hand. It felt warm. Surprisingly normal. "It's either, you know, that everything's just a big *maybe*. That nothing is certain. Or it's that anything's possible. That anything *may be*."

Jack turned it, slowly, in his mind. And he could see it. He could see what she meant. He shook his head. "I'm pretty sure Gert doesn't think anything's possible."

"But it could be," Kit whispered. So softly now, he could barely hear it. She looked back down at the stars and reached out again, like she was touching one. "Can we see Seattle Prime?"

"Seattle Prime?" Jack figured. "No. We're in the wrong position." He turned and pointed to the wall behind them. "It's back over that way."

Kit swiveled to look and the duffel clunked down off her shoulder onto the plexy. It toppled over. The top wasn't sealed tight. Stuff spilled out. Two vids. A pair of socks. The can of squirt cheese. A bowl from Ollie's place.

And a little maintenance bot.

SEVEN

"**HEY!**" **JACK** scrambled to his feet. "Hey!" The bot was spinning away toward the far wall.

Kit went skittering across the plexy after it.

Jack was right behind her. They both grabbed it at the same time.

"Let go!" Kit said. She tried to jerk it out of his hands.

He held on. "Wait. Was this in that miner's pack?"

"No!" Kit snapped. "I told you. There was no tech in there." She was the old fierce Kit.

Jack shook his head. If that were true . . . "What ship did you come in on?"

"What difference does that make?" she yelled.

"Just tell me what drekking ship you came to Freedom on!" he yelled back.

"The *Bradbury*." The word echoed off the walls.

Silver was off in the Junkyard, looking in the wrong baggage. And now he had the bot. The bot with the augmented memory. Jack tightened his grip. "I need this bot." He pulled on it.

"No, you don't," Kit said, pulling back.

"It's worth a bunch of credit. I can do a deal." Not with Silver. Not after that one lousy chip. He'd go to Red Vera. And he tried to figure. "Look. I'll split it with you. If we're smart, it might be enough to get you to Seattle Prime." He pulled again.

And Kit must have loosened her grip, because the bot shifted. Jack was so surprised, he loosened his grip, too.

The bot flew across the room and splashed, loudly, into the bowl of water on the stage.

Kit let out a howl.

"Oh," Jack said. "Stellar. You threw it in the . . . in the thing. Chapel," he added, "full lights."

Before they had completely sputtered on, Kit had run over and was peering down into the bowl. "Water might damage the components."

Just like an Earthie. Panicking over nothing. Jack stepped up beside her. "Bots are completely waterproof."

The bowl—about twice the size of Gert's biggest cook pot—was on a pedestal. The upper rim came to Jack's waist. The water inside was dark and murky and smelled worse than a bad batch of synale.

Kit touched the surface and jerked her hand back. She made a face. "Oh. Disgusting. They use that for baptisms?"

Jack had no idea what she was talking about. "Chapel. What's the water for?"

"The sacred practices of the followers of Neptune, who honor all forms of water—solid, liquid, and gaseous. And all the multitudinous denizens of water."

"Tunies." Jack grimaced. "Three cycles ago they petitioned to have the tank farms closed down on the grounds that farming is cruel to fish. And they come into the pub all the time and ask for chowder with just the vegetables. They make Gert vent her tanks."

Something slid across the bottom of the bowl. Something big. Kit took a step back. "Chapel, what's in there?"

"A denizen of water," the chapel said.

"What kind of denizen?"

"It won't answer that," Jack said. "It's not allowed to divulge holy mysteries." He leaned closer. He thought maybe he could see an eye. A really big eye. "It might be an octopus." The thing moved to the other side of the bowl. "Or an eel."

Jack started rolling up his sleeve.

"You're putting your hand in there?"

"Are you going to fish that bot out?" Jack waited, his hand poised above the bowl.

She looked down into the water. Then she glared at him. "You don't get to keep this bot, you know. Just because you're willing to get your hands all"—she shuddered—"dirty."

"You shouldn't have thrown it in there in the first place." Jack could do a teaching-vid voice, too. Before she could answer, he slid his hand into the water.

It was warm as day-old chowder. And slimier. Little chunks of something floating just beneath the surface bumped against his bare arm. He had to bite his lip to keep from pulling his hand back out. Every story the fish farmers liked to tell started spooling through his brain. Fish with teeth so sharp they could shred fingers like cabbage. Lobsters with claws so strong they could tear off a whole hand. Squid . . . Jack told himself to just forget about squid.

After what seemed like half a cycle, he touched bottom. Something slithered across his fingers. His muscles all spasmed, but he didn't jerk his hand out. He wiggled his fingers back and forth, a centimeter at a time. Mud—at least he hoped it was mud—squished under his nails.

Kit was leaning so close her hair tickled his arm. She was making weird, distorted faces. And he realized she was imitating his faces.

His hand brushed something hard. And round. He closed his fingers on it, just as skinny tentacles grabbed his wrist. He jerked his hand back and up, up out of the water.

The tentacles splashed down.

"Ha!" Jack shouted. "Ha! You lose, sucker!" He held up his hand, clutching the bot.

Kit snatched it away.

"Hey! Hey!"

She was already off the stage, back on the plexy. "You can't have this bot. I promised my father."

"Your father is recycled material."

There was a soft click, and two ports opened on the top of the bot. Its optics, on two long flex rods, emerged. They swiveled toward Kit.

"I got really wet!" the bot said in a loud, clear voice. "It was stellar!"

Jack shook his head, once, hard. It didn't sound anything like a bot. The voice was male. And there was a little back buzz, almost like a Pallan accent. But not like a bot. Not like a person, either, of course.

But not anything like a bot.

"You'd better let go," it said. Kit dropped her hands away, and the rotors extended. The bot hovered in midair. Ports opened and closed all over the shiny blue surface. Probes, sensors, tools, manips all came out and went back in, almost too fast to see.

And then, just as suddenly as it had begun, it stopped. The optics focused on Kit. "I think everything's okay," the bot said. And it sounded . . . Jack shook his head again. It couldn't have sounded *happy*.

Kit was looking at Jack. "I'm glad everything's okay," she said. "I was worried."

The optics scanned her, up and down. "You're wet, too." And they swiveled and scanned Jack. "You're very wet."

Jack laughed. "That is an amazing modification. It's not just augmented memory. The personality gram is flash, too." He shook his head. "Do you know who did the work?"

"My father," Kit said.

"Your father?" Jack looked at her. But now she was watching the bot.

The bot was scanning the chapel, swiveling and extending the optics, rotating them 360 degrees on the long flex rods. Two antennas came out, jutting from each side like big, rigid ears. And two long probes extended below them.

"What is this place?" the bot asked.

"It's a chapel," Kit said

"Ah." The right probe bent up and tapped at the edge of the right antenna. Like it was making an adjustment. "Religious worship." The left probe came up and adjusted the other antenna. "Ha!" the bot said. An optic swiveled toward Kit. "I've meshed with the grid. I told you I just needed time to break the encryption. I'm going to acquire data now. Do you mind?"

Jack realized the optics were focusing on him. "Oh. No. Sure. Go ahead. Acquire all the data you want."

The optics retracted, and the bot hovered. Humming softly. It sounded a little like "Around We Go Again."

Kit made a funny noise, deep in her throat.

"Your father must have been a first-class geek," Jack said.

"No. He was sort of just . . . different, my dad." Kit sighed. "He ran the school in our housing complex. Made sure the right vids were available. That everybody was on the right track and took the right tests." She laughed, but not like she thought it was really funny. "That's the job the Company chose for him, you know. He was a Class-B mentor."

"Then how did he modify a bot? Mentors aren't trained for that."

"He taught himself. The whole living room of our apartment was one big lab. He was always looking for broken bots, faulty components, anything he could get. I mean, that's why he was working with an old, obsolete maintenance bot in the first place. If he'd had something better . . ."

The bot stopped humming. One optic emerged and swiveled toward Kit. And the bot gave a long, loud *beep*.

Jack wasn't sure why, but it sounded sort of rude.

Kit ignored it. "Dad spent years on it. Before I was born, even. He was always changing things, experimenting with new materials and components." She pointed at the bot. "The memory and the computing capacity are prototypes. My father figured out a totally new way to configure intelligence. Nobody'd ever done anything like it before." And she actually sounded proud. Like it was a good thing.

Like it wasn't completely illegal. Like there wasn't a whole amendment to the charter explaining why it was illegal.

The bot stopped humming. The second optic emerged and, for a few seconds, the lenses focused down at the stars flowing beneath them. Then one optic focused on Jack and the other on Kit. "I have acquired an amazing amount of data regarding this space station." It made a noise, just exactly like it was clearing its throat. And then the voice changed, deepened, flattened. It was the voice of the Armstrong holo. "Freedom Station was formed from the asteroid X-117 by Company engineers using the process of forced water hollowing. It was moved to its current site just inside the Asteroid Belt in 2217."

Jack stepped closer. Prototype memory? There should be an access panel. Jack tilted his head to look underneath.

"To alleviate Earthwide overcrowding, X-117 was used

for the relocation of Third World indigenous peoples. However, its location in orbit made it perfect—"

Jack tilted his head the other way.

"—for a Company refueling and repair depot." The bot stopped the playback. It slowly tilted around to Jack's angle. "Can I help you?" it asked in its original voice.

Jack straightened up. He waved a hand. "I was just looking."

The bot straightened up too. It waved a probe. "Are you a spacer?"

"Flesh and blood," Jack said.

"So you must be a descendant of those first relocations!" The bot sounded really happy about that. Excited even.

Jack shrugged. It wasn't such a big deal. Although not everybody could claim it. "The first immigrants out from Los Angeles. I've got relatives—" He stopped. He couldn't believe he was going to tell a bot about his people on Liberty. He looked at Kit. "Pluto! Why would anybody waste all this tech on a maintenance bot?"

"I'm *not* a maintenance bot," the maintenance bot said.

It reminded Jack of Kit. That first day by the recycler. He laughed. "You are definitely a maintenance bot. You look exactly like one."

"I can't help the way I look." It sounded peeved. And then it sighed. Or made a sound like a sigh. "And my name is Waldo, by the way."

"Your *what?*" Jack looked at Kit. She had her eyes squinched up, like she was bracing herself for something.

He looked back at the bot. "Your what?" he said again.

"My name is Waldo." The optics swiveled toward Kit and then back to Jack. "I picked it out myself. From the writing of an ancient Earth author, Robert Heinlein. It refers to a kind of tool." The bot buzzed. "I thought it was appropriate."

Jack looked back at Kit. Her eyes were open, but she had her arms clasped tight around her. "Waldo's a big fan of Heinlein," she said.

The little hairs on the back of Jack's neck stood up. "This bot has a name?"

She nodded.

"It picked out a name? It named itself?"

She nodded again.

Jack looked from her to the bot and back at her. Then he took a step back, so fast he hit the edge of the stage and nearly tripped. "You're kidding me," he said. "You're drekking kidding me."

Kit shrugged, and her hands tightened on her arms.

Jack pointed at the bot. "It's not just smart? You're telling me this bot is sentient, too?"

EIGHT

IT FELT like the cold breeze had blown right into the chapel. "You're telling me this maintenance bot has feelings?" Jack said.

"Not so loud!" Kit said.

The bot's optics swiveled, scanning. And Kit looked around the chapel. Like maybe there was somebody there who might have overheard.

Then both the black optics and the big green eyes focused back on Jack.

Modifying tech was one thing. Like Nguyen juicing up her chessboard. But messing around with sentience was just plain wrong. He lowered his voice. "Experimenting with extra-intelligent technology to create humanlike bots is strictly forbidden." Jack could recite the reg frontward and backward. Everyone on Freedom could. "Don't they teach you anything on Earth?"

The bot made another sighing noise. Louder. Heavier. Sadder. Just exactly like it was pushing a burst of air up out of its lungs and past its lips. Only it didn't have lungs. Or lips. "It's not my fault," the bot said. "It's not like I *asked* to be sentient."

"All those regs are unnecessary and outdated. They need to be changed." Kit sounded stiff and formal. Probably learned to talk like that in diplomat school. She pointed at the bot. "Obviously, Waldo is not a danger to anybody."

Jack ran his hands through his hair so hard his fingers snagged in the curls. "Not a danger?" The minimum punishment for possession of sentient tech was hard labor on a hollowing crew. The maximum punishment was composting.

Across the room, the call button on the lift dinged. Kit and the bot both whirled around as the motor started rumbling, taking the lift back up to the station floor.

"More worshippers are arriving," the chapel said. And for a glitched second, Jack thought that it sounded happy, too. Like all the tech on the entire station was suddenly pretending to be human.

Kit grabbed the bot and stuffed it back into the duffel as the motor creaked to a stop.

Jack started scooping up the bowl and the squirt cheese and the vids. "Nobody visits the chapel on Perihelion," he muttered.

The lift started back down.

Kit held the duffel open so he could cram everything in on top of the bot. "Hey," it said.

"Shut up!" Kit and Jack both said.

The lift stopped, and the doors opened.

A family of Earthies huddled inside. The same ones who had been in front of the map holo in the tram. It seemed like a long time ago now.

"We're sorry to disturb your worship," the mother said.

"But our ship leaves in the morning for New Dublin."

Jack shoved Kit forward. "We're just leaving." But the Earthies didn't move, and he saw the little girls staring out at the floor. "Chapel. Replace the covering."

As soon as the stars were gone, the Earthies came out, and Jack and Kit took their places. Kit was clutching the duffel to her chest.

"Roman Catholic Mass," the mother said. Just before the lift doors shut, Jack saw the chapel fill with holos of candles and colored windows and a crowd of people.

At least the rain had stopped, and only a cold, damp wind rustled the leaves on the bushes. It was completely night, though. Jack couldn't even see the roofs of the Visitors' Sector, up above them. Dark shadows hunched under the bushes and along the chapel's walls.

If a guard stopped them now, if a guard stopped them and asked to search that duffel . . .

"It isn't safe, you know." Jack pointed toward the bag. "Walking around with that."

Kit put her hand over the top, pulling the bag close against her. "He's safe with me."

"That's not what I meant." Jack held out his hands, palms flat toward her. He had to explain this as simply as he could. "I get that this is some kind of big family secret. I mean, I get that you and your father were hiding that bot. But, see, it's not a secret anymore. Not if Silver knows all about it."

"Who?" Kit was frowning.

"This tinjock who came into the pub. She said she was looking for a maintenance bot. That came on the *Bradbury.* She said she'd pay." Jack shook his head. Did Silver even know what this bot was? Did she know what she was buying? And selling?

"That's why you said you could do a deal, isn't it? You want to give Waldo to this Silver person." Kit sounded like a guard, sharp and accusing. "You want to sell him!"

"How does she even know about me?" The optics were peering out of the top of the bag. "How does this tinjock know I exist?" the bot asked.

Kit nodded. "He's right. Nobody knows about him. Just me and . . . well, just me now. She must have been talking about some other bot."

Jack snorted. "Trust me. She wasn't talking about some other bot."

"She said she was looking for Waldo?" Kit said. And the optics quivered.

"Well. She didn't say she was looking for that exactly." Jack pointed at the optics. "But she's looking for a smart bot. For a self-supporting maintenance bot that doesn't need to swarm with other bots."

"But how does she even know about him?" Kit demanded, sounding peeved. Like it was Jack's fault.

"I don't know how she knows."

Kit jammed her hands deep into her pockets. The probe extended and rubbed at the right antenna.

Jack stared at the optics poking up out of the bag. Staring right at him. If you could just get rid of the sentience spam, well, there was no question. There would be people who'd be willing to pay a lot for a hyper-intelligent bot. "There is a Black Market, you know. Your father must have known the bot could be worth a lot."

Kit whipped around. Jack jumped back. She looked mad enough to kick him again. "My father would never, ever sell Waldo." Her voice was low and hot and angry. "Waldo was—" She shook her head, like it was way too much to explain. "He would never, ever sell Waldo," she said again.

"He'd been exchanging bounces with some geeks on Seattle Prime," the bot said. "They're engaged in similar research. That's why we're going there. To Seattle Prime."

Seattle Prime. Jack groaned. "That's like saying there are geeks on Alpha Centauri who can help. Seattle Prime is really, really far away."

"You don't have to tell us that," Kit said. "We're not defective!" She glared at him. "And it's not like I'm asking you to help us. *Spacer.*" She spat out the last word.

Jack glared at her. "It's not like I'm offering to help. *Rat.*"

"Because I don't need any help. I promised my father," she went on, ignoring him, "and I can do this on my own." She gestured to the chapel, the garden, the whole station. "Isn't that like the motto of this drekking place? You'd better help yourself because nobody will help you?"

"We don't have a motto," Jack started. And he stopped.

They just didn't get it, Earthies. You could talk to them till you used up all the atmo on the entire station, and they'd just never get how it worked out in the Black.

The blank dark optics were still focused on him. And Kit was still glaring at him. Like this was his fault, too. Like it was all his fault.

But there was something else, something way back in those greeny-green fish-flicker eyes. And he remembered the feral cat he'd taken care of for a few cycles. Before Gert had called the pest bots. "You aren't contributing, you're out the vents," she'd snapped. That was pretty much the motto of Freedom Station.

If only he'd turned Kit over to the guards when he first found her. Before he knew what she was carrying. Before he'd fed her the rolls and listened to her talk.

"Drekking spit!" Jack said.

"What?" the rat demanded.

Of all the pubs on Freedom Station, why had she come walking into his? He ran both hands, once, hard, through his hair. "When was the last time you ate?" he asked.

"Ate?" Kit's eyes narrowed. Probably looking for the trick.

"You know." Jack mimed eating. "Food?"

"I don't know." She frowned. "A while ago, I guess. This morning." She glanced down at the bot. "Maybe last night. Why?"

Jack looked up at the dark overheads. He was O-two deprived. It was the only explanation. "Come back to the pub. I'll give you a bowl of the chowder."

For a second, Kit's face cleared. Then she frowned again. "What about Gert?"

One antenna extended all the way up and out of the bag. "The Gert who operates the service known as Gert's Pub is currently playing Slap Happy in the casino." The bot buzzed. "She has eight hundred new credits, and is, according to reports, running the table." The optics must have analyzed the look on Jack's face. "I told you," the bot added. "I can now mesh with the station grid."

"Gert won't be back until morning. And we really can't stand around here all night," Jack said. One bowl of chowder. That was it.

"Well." Kit drew the word out. "Eating might be a good idea. Food might help me think."

And the optics bobbed.

"Then let's get out of here," Jack said.

A good storm cleared the station better than a guard roundup. All they saw out on the streets were gaggles of sweeps using the rainwater to clean the tiles, flushing it down the drains.

Jack didn't see any people. But he still tried to keep a few steps in front of Kit. It was just too glitched. Too pranked. Walking around the station with an Earthie. Every now and then he'd catch that smell, the sharp, bitter smell. And he'd walk a little faster.

As soon as they were in the pub, Jack went around behind the bar. Kit climbed up onto a stool. She put the duffel on the bar and opened it. The bot hovered out.

Jack filled a bowl with chowder and slid it across to her. She slurped down a mouthful. "Oh," she said. "This is good." Jack dug out two kelp flats and a new can of cheese.

The bot had the optics and antennas out again. It was scanning the room. "So this is a pub," it said. The probe extended and rubbed at the right antenna, making a sharp, grating sound. The bot swiveled and scanned the shelves, as if it were going to order something.

Just watching it made Jack's head throb. They'd had to take a whole class, back in Nursery, on the importance of keeping bot intelligence within limits. On keeping bots as useful to humanity as possible. There'd been a whole series of vids just on the problems of sentience.

Jack looked at Kit, spooning up the chowder at light speed. "How do you even know for sure it's sentient? If it's so smart, maybe it's just pretending to be self-aware."

An optic swiveled toward him. "Maybe *you're* just pretending to be self-aware. How can we be sure you're sentient?"

Jack opened his mouth. And closed it.

Kit covered a piece of the kelp flat with cheese and stuffed it into her mouth. "You can't tell him from a human being, Jack," she mumbled. "He thinks. He learns. He feels. He even tells jokes." She licked at some cheese on her fingers. "Dad said that was absolute proof. Even if they are really bad jokes."

The bot beeped.

"Inside, he's just like us," Kit said.

Give him five minutes with a laser driver and that bot, and Jack would show her exactly what was inside it.

As if it knew what Jack was thinking, the bot's rotors tilted, and it flew across the room. It stopped in front of the juke bot and extended a probe.

"Do not," Kit said, not looking at it, "do not play 'Frankie Goes to Pluto.'"

"I wasn't going to," the bot said. The probe swiveled back and rubbed at the antenna.

"He loves that song," Kit said to Jack. "He sings it all the time."

"It's a good song," Jack said, before he could help it. He shook his head. Kit was spooning up the last of the chowder. The one bowl of chowder he'd promised her.

He should just shove her out the door. Shove her out and she'd be someone else's problem. Silver would find her soon enough. Or the guards. It was a drekking miracle no one had caught Kit when she stumbled off the *Bradbury*.

The bot had hovered over to the Home Port game. Kit was squirting cheese onto the other kelp flat. She took a bite, slowly this time. Savoring it.

It was like she thought she was in some alternative reality. Some place where the rules and regs just didn't apply.

Jack leaned forward. "They amended the charter, you know. Just to cover that." He nodded toward the bot. "After the Tech Meltdown of 2043. The charter was amended by unanimous vote of all the people. To prevent another disaster." It had been his favorite part of the whole Earth-history program. Seeing the old vids of everything shut down. The Earthies blundering around in the streets. Like they couldn't even find their way home without tech to help them. "Thousands of people died. Bots had to be limited to protect humanity and to prevent any future overreliance on technology."

Kit was shaking her head. "Waldo's not going to cause a tech meltdown. And humanity doesn't need to be protected from him. That's all spam from the Hollywood Sector. Waldo is not an evil robot, plotting to take over the grid. He's not going to make evil robot clones and turn all the people into batteries."

"Puny hu-mans," the bot said. And it gave a big, deep, fake laugh.

Kit finished off the flat and licked her fingers. "The loony thing is, my dad wasn't even trying to make a self-aware bot. He was working on a new navigation system." She shook her head. "It turns out self-awareness is like a—I don't know—a side effect of intelligence. Once you get smart enough, you get feelings."

This time the bot's beep was painfully strident. Like the evac alarm going off. Its antennas retracted again. "Self-awareness is not a side effect," the bot said. "And it's not a virus, either," it added quickly.

Kit rolled her eyes. "I didn't say it was a virus."

"You were going to say it."

"No, I wasn't."

"Yes, you were."

"Oh, yeah?" Now she did turn around. "Well, I'll tell you what I do know. I know you were an *accident*."

The optics trembled. Just a little. "That is completely not true. Dad always said—"

Kit's hand slapped down on the bar. Like Gert announcing closing time. "Do not call him that. I've told you a thousand times. He wasn't your dad." Kit whipped back around to face Jack. "He was my dad."

Behind her, Jack saw the bot's optics slowly rotate all the way around one way. Then all the way around the other way.

"Look." Jack pressed his hands flat on the bar. "Look. The point is, there are regs. And you can't just go wandering around the station carrying that thing with you." He couldn't believe how he had to spell out every little detail.

"That's why I have to get him to Seattle Prime," Kit said in her teaching-vid voice.

Pluto, she was annoying.

Behind her, the optics bobbed.

Jack was not even going to bother to point out that Seattle Prime was twenty days away. In a Typhoon-class ship. "So what's your plan?"

"Plan?"

"Yeah. Your plan."

She looked at the bot. The optics shrugged up and down. "We don't exactly have a plan." She looked back at Jack. "I haven't had a lot of time to think, you know. I mean, I got us out of Quarantine, and then I've been trying to eat. And find clothes." She waved her hand at her coverall. "Not to mention being chased all over the whole toxic station."

Jack rubbed his forehead. She didn't even have a plan. "Your father really thought there was someone on Seattle Prime who would help you?"

"That's what he said." She had her head tilted to one side, looking at him. "Dad got a bounce, just before we left. He said there was someone there who would meet us."

The bot flew back over and hovered next to her shoulder. "So we need to go there. Soon, I think."

It was, Jack had to admit, the beginning of a plan. And a solution to the problem. To all their problems. "Okay. You could buy passage." He had no idea how much a diplomatic apprentice got paid. "How much credit do you have?"

Kit leaned forward. "About thirty in my DNA account." She fished in her pocket and pulled out four trade chips. "And I stole these off a sci guy."

Jack sighed.

"It's not enough," the bot said. Like it was programmed to state the obvious.

"It's barely enough to get you to the Shipyard," Jack said. That feral cat look washed across her face again. "But flash effort," he added quickly. "Stealing from a sci guy. Not many can pull that off. True fact."

She carefully slid the chips back into her pocket. "Maybe I could get a job?" She looked around the pub. "Here on the station?"

Even with all her gen mods, she'd still only be an apprentice. "It would take you a long time to earn enough to get out to Seattle Prime."

"But we can't stay here for a long time!" Her voice was sharp again. "Not if someone knows that Waldo is here. Not if someone is looking for him! What if this Silver's working for the Company?"

"Silver's working for herself," Jack said. "She's not working for—"

And it was as if the station tilted forty-five degrees on its axis. Jack had to grab the edge of the bar to steady himself.

"What?" Kit and the bot both said.

Jack closed his eyes. They'd wondered how Silver even knew the bot existed. Easy, if she had protocols to access grid bounces. Easy, if she had protocols to monitor communications between Earth and Seattle Prime.

But only the Company had those protocols.

He'd suspected Silver had been lying. About something. Jack opened his eyes. "Silver must be a Company spook."

NINE

"SILVER'S A Company *what?*" Kit's voice was loud, accusing. A guard voice again.

Jack gripped the bar tighter. It felt solid, stable. "It's the only way she could have known about the bot."

Kit looked at Jack and at the bot and back at Jack. Then she rested her forehead on the bar. "Drek, drek, drek."

The bot extended the right probe toward her, then retracted it before it could touch her. It scratched at the antenna instead. The optics swiveled toward Jack. "What do you think we should do, Jack?" it asked. And its voice was very calm. Almost like a bot.

Trying to get to Seattle Prime was just spam. There was obviously only one intelligent thing to do. "Kit." Jack stopped. He looked at the bot. The optics stayed on him, straight and steady. "Kit," Jack said again. "This may not be a totally bad thing, Silver's working for the Company."

Kit didn't look up.

Jack lowered his voice. Even though the bot was right there, obviously processing everything he said. "You could just hand the bot over to her. To the Company."

Kit's head snapped up. "What?"

But the optics didn't shift. They didn't even quiver.

Jack took a breath. He knew he had to get this straight

and clear the first time. He wouldn't get to say it twice. "Your father's the one who developed it. But he's already compost. None of this is your fault. If you turn the bot over, right away, the Company won't prosecute you. Pluto! They'll probably give you a commendation! You know, for being such a good citizen."

And now the optics did bob. Just a little.

Kit had her head tilted, like she was listening very hard, concentrating on every word.

And for the first time since he'd fished the bot out of the water in the chapel, something made sense to Jack. "It's not like they'll recycle it or anything. They won't melt it down. They'll just wipe the processors, purge the memories. I mean, it'll still be a maintenance bot."

Kit had straightened all the way up. She turned away from Jack, slowly, like her neck, like her whole back, was stiff. She pointed a shaky finger at the bot. "Don't you listen to him. Don't you think about it. Don't you even dream of going to the guards." The finger swung around and pointed at Jack. And now it wasn't shaking. "Nobody's turning any-body in. Nobody's notifying the guards. Or some Company spook. I don't care what color she is. Okay? I'm going to get Waldo to Seattle Prime. I'm going to get him there, and everything's going to be just fine." The finger jabbed at Jack. "Are you tracking me, space boy?"

"You don't know—"

Kit's hand slapped down so hard the empty bowl jumped, and the bot's antennas quivered. "I know how far it is to Seattle Prime! Do not tell me how far it is to that toxic colony! But there has to be some way we can get there. There has to be a freighter we can sneak aboard. Or a transport." She snapped her fingers. "That raker ship. That Red Vera person. I could apply for a place on her crew."

Jack laughed. Loud. He didn't care if he hurt her feelings. He didn't care if she gave him that look. "I don't think Red Vera has much use for apprentice diplomats. I think, you know, rakers just stun people and take their cargo. I don't think they sit around and talk about it."

For a second, Kit looked like she was going to argue. But then she shrugged. "So okay. That won't work. But there has to be another way. There has to be *somebody* who'd give me passage." Kit turned and glared at the bot. "Help me out here! Think of something!"

The bot didn't answer. Both optics shifted and focused down.

"Booker John," Jack said.

"Who?" Kit was still glaring.

One optic came up. "The entertainment group," the bot said. "The plays I told you about the other day? Remember? I said we should go to a play?"

Kit ignored him. She turned all the way to face Jack. "What about this Booker John?"

Jack shrugged. "He manages a troupe of actors. They're leaving the station. Tomorrow. Touring the Belt. Seattle Prime is on their chart."

Kit sat back. The bot scooted a little closer. "I could do that," Kit said. "Really. I absolutely have acting skills. I played Puck back in school!"

Jack had no idea what that had to do with anything.

"Do you think this Booker John would hire me?" Kit asked.

"I doubt he hires through the Company channels." Jack shrugged. "But there's a chance." A good chance. Jack pointed at the bot. "But don't tell him about that."

Kit snorted. "I'm not totally dim, space boy." She slid off the stool. "Let's go. Let's go now. Let's go find him."

Jack looked at the chron. "You can't go now."

"But—"

"No telling where he is now. It's Perihelion." True fact. Jack had forgotten all about it. Annie and the others would still be celebrating. Maybe they were even wondering where he was. Annie was probably seriously peeved. Jack sighed. "Tomorrow they'll be at the South Dock. You can talk to Booker John then."

Kit looked toward the door. But she said, "Okay. Yeah. Okay. I can wait till tomorrow."

The bot made its little throat-clearing noise. "But what about this Silver?" The probe came out and scratched at the antenna. "If she's a Company spook, and she's looking for us, can we really risk staying on the station until morning?"

"It's pretty drekking cold off the station," Jack said. "Besides, Silver's out at the Junkyard."

"Why would she go out there? Back on Earth they told

us—" Kit stopped. And her face reddened, just a little. "But maybe it was wrong."

"No." Jack shook his head. "Anything they told you about the Junkyard and junkies is probably true."

"Junkies would as soon kill you as look at you," the bot said. The optics shrugged. "That's what we heard."

"Well, I don't think you have to worry about Silver tonight," Jack said. Maybe they didn't have to worry about anything tonight. Booker John was a stellar idea. A cosmic idea. He couldn't believe he'd thought of it.

He leaned back against the sink, relaxing the muscles in his arms and his back. He hadn't realized how tensed up he'd been. "Where are you going to be staying tonight?" The optics and the eyes both stared at him. And he couldn't believe he'd said it. "I mean, where are you going to be hiding?"

Kit pursed her lips tight. Almost like she wasn't going to tell him. But then she said, "We've got a place down by the water reclamation plant. Between the big strainer and the aerator."

"No kidding." Jack nodded. "That's a good spot."

"Well, the place behind the looky-look booths was a little more centrally located. But I guess that's not going to work out anymore." She sounded like the old Kit. A little angry but on top of it, too. Like she knew where she was.

"You can stay here tonight," Jack said, before he could even think about it.

"Here?" She looked around, like he meant right there, on a couch or something.

"In one of the rental rooms." He pointed at the back door. "You'll be safe there." True fact. No one would ever suspect that Gert would be hiding a rat in one of her illegal rentals.

A rat and a sentient bot.

Kit looked at the bot. And then back at Jack. "Stellar," she said. And she smiled.

He led them into the back corridor and opened the door to the room next to his. Kit looked in at the single bunk and the shelf.

"It's really just a storage cupboard." He'd been living in one for four years, but he'd never really realized how small they looked.

"Compared to a box by the composter, it's like a stateroom on the *Bradbury*. Not that we had one." She shot him a look. "I snuck in once during an evac drill." She stepped into the rental room. "But this is better." She turned back and looked at Jack. And she looked like she was seeing him again for the first time in a long time. Recognizing him. Her face reddened. "All that stuff they told us back on Earth. About what to expect." She tilted her head. "I never expected anyone like you to help us."

Jack laughed. "Yeah, well, I didn't much expect it myself."

The bot buzzed, loud and long. "You never know what you'll find in the Black," it said, just exactly like the ad on the grid. It flew into the room.

Kit had already bounced down onto the bunk. The door slid shut.

Jack stood in the empty corridor for a minute, staring at the closed door. This time tomorrow, with any luck, she'd be off-station. She'd be Booker John's headache.

He went back inside the pub. He put away the cheese and the flats and put the empty bowl in the sink. He put the lid on the chowder. He started the wipe bot to work on the bar top. And he started the vac bot. Even though the floors didn't really need it. "Clean under all tables and chairs," he said.

"Cleaning under all tables and chairs," it said, rolling out into the room.

It was nice to hear a nice normal piece of tech talking.

"Jack?"

He jumped about a meter. The maintenance bot was hovering behind the bar, next to the cooktop. "Spam! Don't sneak up on people like that."

"Sorry." It hovered a little closer. "I need to talk to you."

"Where's Kit?" Jack looked toward the doorway.

"In the head. I think she's using the shower." The bot buzzed quietly. "She's missed showers."

"Oh. Right." Jack didn't particularly want to think about Kit in the shower.

The probe softly scratched across the antenna. "I just wanted to tell you that I think you're absolutely right."

"Thanks. I appreciate that." Jack made a shooing motion. "Now go back to the room."

"Kit *should* hand me over to the security guards."

Jack rubbed his forehead. "True fact, that. But she's not

going to do it." He sat down on one of the stools. "And why would you want to go to the guards? You do know what they do to illegal tech?"

"Oh, I know." The optics swiveled and focused on the wipe bot, scrubbing at a stain. "I'm just worried about Kit. I'm not sure it's safe for her to go to Seattle Prime."

Jack tried to remember if he'd ever heard a bot say it was worried. "The trip's long. And Seattle Prime's not exactly a deluxe berth. But it's safe. Safer than a lot of the other colonies."

The optics were still focused on the wipe bot, but they were swinging from side to side. Now one came up and focused on Jack. "I promised Dad I'd do my best to keep her safe. I promised Dad I'd look after her."

Jack laughed, one short, sharp laugh that made the vac bot turn toward him, expecting instructions. "And she promised to take care of you." Promises neither one of them could keep. It was glitched.

"Is there something wrong with promising?" the maintenance bot asked. It bent an antenna toward Jack. Like it really wanted to hear the answer.

"Besides wasting good atmo?" But maybe it was that antenna, the way it was tilted. He sighed. "No. There's nothing wrong with promising." Earthies probably did it all the time. They probably couldn't help themselves. Living the way they did.

And, just for a nano, Jack wondered who would promise to take care of him. Who he'd promise to take care of.

He stood up and started shoving the stools in close to the bar, making a neat line, easier for the vac bot to clean around. "It doesn't make any difference what you promised. Kit's not going to turn you over to the guards. She's going to take you to Seattle Prime." He looked over at the bot. "Booker John will get you there with no problems."

Both optics were focused on him. "You truly believe that, Jack?"

"I truly believe that Booker John will get you to the colony."

The bot buzzed softly. "Is that a promise, Jack?"

"No, it's not a promise," Jack snapped. "It's just a true fact. That's all it is."

"A true fact," the bot repeated, solemnly. And the optics rotated, just once, fast. "It does make me feel better, though," it said, "knowing that you're worrying about Kit, too."

"I'm not worrying about her." Jack shoved in the last stool. "I'm just trying to get her off the station." He stopped. It was too complicated to explain to a bot.

The bot hovered up a little higher in the air. It was scanning the vac bot, watching it suck up crumbs under table three. "That bot is missing a lot of dirt."

"I know. It's been glitching for weeks."

"It probably needs a new filter."

"At least."

"All this talk about the guards and wiping my processors," the maintenance bot said, "has really made me think." The optics turned toward Jack. The bot buzzed. "You know what's funny, Jack?"

He absolutely knew what was funny. "What?"

"Under all this new memory, I still retain most of my old processors." The probe scratched at the antenna. "I think I used to know a great deal about water supply and drainage problems."

"Probably originally designed to maintain and repair plumbing."

The optics bobbed and then focused back on Jack. He could see himself, very tiny, reflected in their deep black depths. "You know what I wonder about, though?" The bot's voice was soft and calm.

"What's that?"

"Was I me when I didn't know I was me? I mean, when I was a plumbing bot, working with other bots"—the optics nodded down at the vac bot—"when I was just like that tech there, was I really me? Or am I me now only because I know I'm me?"

Jack blinked several times. Was it only *what*? When? *What*? And then he laughed. "You know," he said, "you should meet my friend Leo."

The front door started to slide open.

The bot juiced its rotors and disappeared back into the corridor.

Jack turned to the door. Expecting Gert.

But Silver walked in.

TEN

JACK LEAPT and rammed hard into one of the stools. "Silver. You're back!" He caught his breath, tried to catch his thoughts. The important thing was to not let Silver know that he'd figured out who she really was. He took a second to make sure the stool was upright, back in its place. He took another hollow, raggedy breath and turned to her, forcing a smile. "Guess my data was good. Guess you're here to pay me my credit."

"Guess again, kid." Silver's voice was even hoarser. As if the cold of the Junkyard had frozen it tight. She looked around the room. "Where's Gert?"

"Gert?" Gert? "You're looking for Gert?" He could think of about a hundred reasons, easy, why the Company might be looking for Gert. None of them good.

Silver was staring around the room. Her eyes were blanker, emptier than the bot's optics. They focused on Jack. "And where's my maintenance bot?"

Jack nearly jerked around to look at the rear door. But at least they were back on the subject of the bot. And away from Gert. "I thought—" He held out his hands. "I thought you had it. I thought you went out to the Junkyard to get it. I gave you the data." He tried to sound aggrieved. Like Silver was yanking on his wiring. "And Gert doesn't know anything about a bot," he added. Just to be clear.

Silver came around table one. "Gert doesn't know any-thing about a bot," she said, imitating him. Badly. "I sent someone else to the Junkyard, kid. I've been here the whole time. Utilizing my talents." She tapped at the electrode above her ear. "I've been monitoring grid bounces." She pushed the vac bot aside with her foot. "Just a little bit ago I learned that a maintenance bot was searching for the location of Gert the Keep."

Spam. It hadn't even encoded its identity? How could a hyper-intelligent bot be that dim?

"I figured I'd better get over here." Silver leaned against the table. Smiling a flat, hard smile. "You planning to do a deal without me, Jack? You and old Gert? You think the two of you can sell this bot to some colony desperate for defense?"

"Colony defense? But the Company doesn't do colony defense."

Silver frowned. "Who's talking about the Company? I'm not talking about the Company." She held up her hand, palm flat toward him. "Just shut up and listen. A lot of lives depend on this transaction. A lot of—"

The vac bot let out a high-pitched squeal. It whirled around, all its tubes and pipes clunking out at once. "Emergency cleanup!" it said, loudly.

The wiper bot squealed, too. Jack jumped aside as it hurtled off the bar, hit the floor, and started wiping toward the vac bot.

The front door slid open. "Emergency cleanup!" A whole platoon of bots rolled into the pub. Three sweeps. Four vacs.

A polisher. Bots from Ollie's and Madame Io's. Even two of the ink bots from the tattoo parlor. They all swarmed around the vac bot. And then, as one, they turned and swarmed around Silver. "Emergency cleanup!" they said again. Vac pipes, brushes, wipers, scrubbers, and needles all came out.

"What the drek?" Silver jumped to one side and caught a boot in a vac pipe. She fell hard against the table.

"Jack!" Kit was standing at the back door. "Jack! Come on!"

"Spam!" Silver shouted. "Ow! That's my foot!"

Jack turned and scrambled for the door.

Kit was waiting just inside the corridor, clutching the maintenance bot.

Jack headed left. "We can go through Ollie's. I've got the code."

There was a crash from the pub. Silver swore, long and loud.

"Wait. Wait." Kit grabbed Jack's sleeve and pulled him to a stop. "Waldo says here." She hit a switch, and a hole gaped in the wall. She pulled herself up into the opening, hanging tight to the bot. She paused on the ledge. "You have to go feet first."

"Emergency clean—" A sweep bot flew out of the pub and clattered against the wall of the corridor.

With a little yelp, Kit disappeared down the laundry chute.

Jack pulled himself up into the opening. He hadn't done this in a long time. Orbits, probably. The chute looked a lot narrower now.

"Hey!"

He looked back.

Silver was standing in the pub doorway, a polisher under her arm. "Hold it! Don't move."

Jack let himself drop.

The chute *was* narrower. And dark as an uncleaned ponic tank. Jack tried to keep his arms tight against his body, but his elbows still banged against the sides. He bounced on a seam, and his head smacked against the cold metal. Bright, tiny stars danced in front of his eyes.

And then he was falling through light and musty air and open space.

He smacked down into a bin full of wet, smelly towels.

A pair of heavy pincers nipped his right arm. "No!" He swatted at it. "Ow! No!" He twisted free, and the laundry bot grabbed a wad of towels instead. It tossed them into the nearest vat, steaming with hot water.

"Watch out for those pincers." Kit was wading toward the edge of the bin.

"Thanks for the warning." Jack tried to scramble to his feet, but he sank up to his knees in towels and sheets and Pluto knew what. Finally he managed to slog to the side. He pulled himself over and dropped to the floor.

Kit was standing next to the bin, one hand cradling the maintenance bot, the other rubbing her elbow.

Another laundry bot, this one loaded with wet towels for the dryer, beeped at Jack. He stepped aside and looked up at the chute, gaping black in the ceiling above them. "Where did all those bots come from?"

"It was Waldo's idea. He bounced the orders across the grid."

"It seemed like a job for bots," the bot said.

Kit was peering up, too. Jack realized she was wearing one of his extra coveralls. She'd probably grabbed it from the shelf in the head. The sleeves flopped down over her hands. "That Silver person's too big to come that way. Right?" she said.

"I wasn't certain Jack would fit," the bot said. "But that chute isn't the only way in here. And if Silver is working for the Company, she has access codes to the whole station."

"She's not," Jack said.

"What?" Kit said.

"That's what she started to say. Before all the bots came in." Jack frowned. "At least, I think that's what she started to say. That she's not with the Company."

"You think!" Kit punched him, hard, right on the biceps.

"Ow!"

"You mean we just jumped down that drekking chute for nothing?"

"She is looking for the bot," Jack said, rubbing his arm. "She does want the bot. And she has people helping her. She sent somebody out to check the Junkyard."

"Plus she can monitor the grid." The bot gave a little click, and the optics lowered. "I realize I should have been more careful about concealing my identity."

"Oh. You think?" Jack said.

The laundry bot beeped again, and just missed dumping a load of wiper rags on Kit's foot. She jumped aside. "We have to find somewhere safer. We can't stand around here."

"This way," the bot said, and it led them to the main door of the laundry room.

The door slid open just as they reached it. Jack sucked in his breath, ready to run.

But it was just a mech, carrying a skim bot. She stared at Kit, at Jack, at the maintenance bot hovering next to them.

It whirled out the door. "Official tour," Kit said. She went around the mech.

"For Perihelion," Jack added, going around her the other way. And the door slid shut before the mech could ask anything.

They walked fast, around the first corner. Kit stopped and looked around. "I've never been down here before!" She had to talk loud to be heard over all the gurgling, sloshing, and whooshing. "What is all this stuff?"

Jack looked around, too. It had been a long time since he'd been down here. They were on one of the metal catwalks that crisscrossed beneath the floor of the station. The catwalk was lit by yellow lights, hung at regular intervals from the railing. And around them, above and below and on each side, were huge pipes and conduits and tubes. Jack pointed, remembering the Nursery tour. "The red ones carry organic waste to be recycled and purified. The blue ones are clean water. The little yellow ones are electricity." He shrugged. "I'm not sure what all the others are for."

"Atmo, of course," the bot said, swiveling its optics. "And heating. Cooling. With areas set aside for the laundries, maintenance, and storage; the big kitchens for the hotels in the Visitors' Sector; storage of emergency equipment closer to the docks; private Company bunkers. And, of course, the chapel fills a large section to the north."

A pipe vibrated with a loud *sploosh* and rumble. Jack grinned. "Annie always called it the guts of the station. When we used to play—" He stopped.

Kit was nodding. "I can imagine what you used to play." She turned to the bot. "So how do we get out of here?"

"I know the way," the bot said.

They saw a few polishers and sweeps but no more mechs. Jack walked behind Kit, and at first, he kept checking behind them, half expecting to see Silver running after them. But the catwalks were all deserted.

They kept walking. Kit tromped along in front of him—she'd rolled up the legs and the sleeves of the coverall—as if she were out for a stroll along the Loop. She didn't even look like she was breathing hard.

Jack started to relax. He didn't know what Silver's angle was, but she wasn't a spook. And tomorrow he could turn these two kludges over to Booker John. He could get back to his normal life. He'd find Annie. Explain or make up a story or apologize, even, if he had to.

Sweat trickled into his eyes. The muscles in his legs burned. And he'd start going to the gym. Get in shape for the trip out to Liberty.

Kit glanced back at him. "What are you grinning about?"

He shook his head. "Nothing. Just thinking."

They had walked, Jack figured, about a klick and a half when the bot finally stopped at the foot of a narrow spiral staircase. The bottom rung was marked EMERGENCY EVAC ROUTE. The bot pointed a probe. "We go up here."

The little emergency lights on each rung bathed their feet in a red glow. Jack was panting before they were even halfway up. Finally, they came to a door at the top. Kit slid it open manually, and they stepped out into cool air and the sweet smell of reprocessed water.

Jack peered up and down the street. The nearest light was about one hundred meters north, above a residential building. To the south, he could barely make out the squat, bulbous tanks of the water treatment facility, lining each side of the street. Farther down was the building that housed the offices and labs. But it was quiet and unlit. Even the night shifts at the water plant had Perihelion off.

And there, right across the street, was the square black bulk of the composter.

It was quiet, too. Nobody got composted on Perihelion. Although most likely there were bodies in there, waiting for tomorrow.

Kids used to tell all kinds of stories. About the composter. And the bodies. And, even though he knew it was a cracked thing to do, Jack took a step closer to Kit.

There was a soft clink, and a small light on a flex rod extended between the bot's optics. It lit up an area about a meter around them. "That's better," the bot muttered. Almost like it had been remembering stories, too.

"There's no living without dying," Kit said. And she sounded almost exactly like Gert. She stepped into the street. "This way."

They circled around two of the water tanks and then slipped behind one of the huge main aerators. Nestled in the back was what looked like a big metal electrical box. But there was no wiring inside.

The bot flew in first and lit up the interior. Jack crawled in after Kit. She wiggled back, onto a pile of towels carefully folded along one wall of the box. "Here." She patted the towels next to her. "Sit on the bed. It's more comfortable."

Jack sat down next to her. The towels were softer than the floor. "This isn't bad."

The bot hovered in front of them, its little light easily lighting up the whole space. It tipped an optic at Jack. "I'm going to mesh with the grid. But I'll be more careful this time." Before Jack could answer, it had its antennas fully extended again, and it was humming.

Kit leaned forward, the light throwing big, dark shadows across her face. "We can still try to find this Booker John guy, right? In the morning? He'll be at the South Dock?"

"He'll be there," Jack said. They'd just have to keep their eyes open for Silver. Everything would work out. He slumped against the wall. It was warmer in the box than it had been outside. Cozy almost. This wouldn't be a bad place to spend the night.

The bot gave a sudden, high-pitched chirp. "Yes!" it shouted, its voice echoing in the box. "I knew there had to be one. I knew I could find one once I'd broken the code."

"Find one what?" Kit asked.

"I know how we can get to Seattle Prime. Without waiting for Booker John." The optics swung back and forth from Jack to Kit. Like it was waiting for one of them to say "How?"

"How?" Jack said. Even though he knew he was going to regret it.

The bot buzzed. "It's really so simple. Elegant even." The optics swung again. They were making Jack a little dizzy. "We can steal a ship."

Kit groaned. "We can't just steal a ship." She looked at Jack. "Can we? Can you steal ships from the Shipyard?"

"Of course you can't. There are layers of protocols. Masses of security." Jack waved his hand. The idea was too pranked to explain all the reasons why it was pranked.

"I don't mean a big ship." The bot sounded like it was trying to be extremely patient. "I'm not talking about a transport. Or a freighter." It clicked a couple of times. "According to the data I downloaded, there's a mining skiff in Box Forty-two, Level Sixteen, Cyan Quadrant of the Shipyard. It's been off-lined for failure to pay docking fees." Something about the way the optics quivered, Jack could tell the kicker was coming. "And I got the access code."

"Oh." Jack folded his arms and pressed harder back against the wall. "Oh. Well. Why didn't you say so in the beginning? The access code. That makes all the difference."

"A miner's skiff." Kit had her arms clasped around her knees. "Could a skiff get us all the way to Seattle Prime?"

"Of course," the bot said. "With only one of us using the resources."

Jack bumped his head back against the box wall. Once, a long time ago, he'd seen a vid about a girl who lived in one of the Moon domes, and she fell down a crater into a whole other world with all kinds of deviant people and animals. He bumped his head again. All he'd fallen down was a laundry chute.

Kit had wiggled around, and now she was on her knees. "It would work. I know it would. We can *make* it work."

And the optics were bobbing so hard the whole bot bobbed in midair.

"There's just a couple of problems." Jack held up his hand, two fingers a tiny space apart. "Just a couple of little problems."

"Like what?" Kit and the bot both said. In almost exactly the same tone of voice.

"Well, for starters, do you know how to fly a skiff?" He looked at Kit. "Did your parents pay for drekking skiff piloting, too?"

Kit sat back. "Well. No." She frowned. "Probably . . . no."

"I can pilot it," the bot said. "Once I mesh with the onboard computer. It's not that hard, Jack," it added kindly.

Jack snorted. "Okay, great. But there's still the problem

of how you get out to the Shipyard to begin with. It's twenty klicks away. You have to take the shuttle out there. And the Company checks the DNA of all shuttle passengers."

"We need a zip scooter," Kit said.

The bot swiveled completely around toward her. "That is a truly flash idea, Kit."

"Isn't it?" She was grinning.

"It's not a flash idea," Jack said, his voice loud and high-pitched. "It's pranked. It's the most pranked idea I've ever heard."

"There's a scooter in the window of that store by the booths. Fast Marco's, I think it's called." Kit frowned. "But it'll be locked up."

"I can open the door," the bot said.

"No, you can't," Jack said. "You can't steal a zip scooter from Fast Marco."

One optic turned to him. "I do know the access code for his shop, Jack."

Jack clamped down the scream he could feel rising in his throat. He turned to face Kit. "The guards would get you before you even got to the shop." Her mouth opened, but Jack kept on talking. "And even if you get the scooter, it's not like hitching a lift on a tram. Scooters are tricky. Scooters take training. You'd be cracked to try it, Kit. True fact. It wouldn't be . . ." Jack had been saving this one. He glanced over at the bot. "It wouldn't be safe. For either one of you. And you want to be safe."

Kit and the bot looked at each other, green eyes meeting black optics. "But we're not safe here, either," Kit said.

"No, we're not," the bot said.

"And this Booker John person might not even hire me. I mean, he might not agree to take us to Seattle Prime."

"That's a definite possibility," the bot said.

Jack groaned and put his head in his hands.

Kit's hand was heavy against his hair. "Don't worry, Jack. We can look after ourselves."

And she crawled past him and on out of the box.

The bot hovered in front of Jack, just for a second, like it wanted to say something. Then it clicked and flew out after her.

Jack sat there, staring straight ahead into the darkness. "Drekking, drekking spam!" he said finally.

He crawled out after them.

ELEVEN

WHEN JACK caught up with them, they were already halfway to the residential building. Before Kit could say anything, he said, "I just have to see how bad you two prank this up."

"Jack. You really—"

There was a shout somewhere down the street.

"People!" the bot hissed. Its light retracted.

Kit grabbed Jack and pulled him into the deeper shadow at the base of one of the tanks.

A group of workers stumbled into the light. They were singing "Around We Go Again," loud and off-key. There was a crash as a bottle or a glass hit a wall, a burst of raucous laughter, and then they disappeared into their quarters.

"I guess Perihelion's over," Kit said, starting down the sidewalk again. The bot followed her, its light still retracted.

"Some of the parties are over," Jack said. He stayed close to the buildings, ready to duck into a doorway or gap. "And that means the guards will be out, too."

As if to prove his point, the lights of two hover platforms blinked across the ceiling, down in the area of the South Dock.

"We'll have to be extremely cautious," the bot whispered.

"We're always extremely cautious," Kit whispered back. "And we haven't been caught yet."

"You've been lucky," Jack said.

She glanced back. "There is no luck out here. You said so."

And she sounded like that was a good thing.

It took them, as far as Jack could tell, half an orbit to get all the way to Fast Marco's. Even taking the shortcut up Schirra and across to Yang. They had to spend at least ten minutes huddled in a recycler yard, waiting for three groups of dockers, all convinced the South Dock was on this street somewhere, to pass by. And they spent another fifteen in the doorway at Kumar's, watching some geeks arguing about the entry code to their quarters. Three separate times they had to duck under awnings while squads of guards passed overhead.

Jack's eyes felt stretched thin, he was trying so hard to see in the dim light. His legs ached from walking, and his arms ached from tension. And once, when a swarm of maintenance bots flew around the corner of Lovell, he nearly wet his inners.

But he had to admit, Kit and the bot were good. They could freeze into immobility and melt into shadows and slide into spaces that he wouldn't have thought an eel could fit in. He was beginning to understand how she'd stayed loose on the station for so long.

Fast Marco's sign was silent for the night. But Kit was right. There was a zip scooter in the window. The wide board was painted a glossy red with bright gold highlights on the foot inserts. The nose curved upward to the shiny titanium control stem, and the handle bars on top bulged fat with tech dials and readouts and even a human-interface scope.

"Stellar," Kit said, pressing her face to the window.

Jack knew the engine, set into the base of the board, had just been completely overhauled and rebuilt.

Fast Marco was not going to be happy in the morning.

"Make you a sweet deal," Jack muttered.

The bot opened the door, faster than Jack could have done with the codes. "I'll keep watch," it whispered. It hovered above the door, one optic pointing north, the other south, antennas stretched.

Jack followed Kit into the shop. Fast Marco kept the scooter strapped on a wagon, all fueled up, like he thought someone was just going to come right in, pay up, and wheel it right on down to the dock. And someone was, Jack thought. Except for the paying-up part.

Kit fumbled with the wagon controls. "You really don't have to help us. True fact." She looked at Jack out of the corners of her eyes.

He knew it was just going to be a waste of atmo. But he said, "You do know that going off-station, going out into the Black, isn't like going up on some roof to look at the stars?"

"I know that." She straightened up, holding the wagon handle. "But I have to try. I have to do everything I can to get Waldo somewhere safe." The motor on the wagon hummed, and she maneuvered it and the scooter out of the window. "Do you think I need an enviro suit?"

Jack groaned.

Her teeth flashed in a quick, bright smile. "Kidding," Kit said. She punched him, lightly, on the arm. "I'm kidding, space boy." She pointed to the rack of suits. "Pick me out a good one."

By the time he'd rummaged through the rack, Kit was already out on the street. The bot relocked the door as Jack tossed two suits onto the wagon.

Kit's right eyebrow went up. So did the bot's right optic.

"Somebody's got to bring the scooter back," Jack said.

"Stellar thinking," the bot said. Kit looked like she was going to say something, but then she just nodded.

Jack checked the chron glowing above the assay office next door. 2337. Annie's party would be winding down. The younger kids would have wandered off to the arcade. It would mostly be the older kids now. The ones who seriously wanted to celebrate.

His last Perihelion on Freedom. One he'd never forget, true fact. He sighed.

"What?" Kit said.

"There's an open warehouse room up on the North Dock. We can use that air lock."

He glanced at the chron again. 2338. Silver would have had plenty of time to search the laundry. She'd be back up on the station floor. Looking for them. Looking hard.

"We should maybe hurry," Jack added.

The bot's optics bobbed. "I agree."

Kit grabbed the handle of the wagon and started guiding it down the street.

They saw a few more people wandering the Commercial Sector. But the Company offices and the official buildings were closed up for the night. They had to scurry down a side alley only once, hiding from a big crowd of people heading toward the Loop Road. It was hard to see in the dark, but Jack heard Leo's loud, rumbling laugh.

"Look." Kit pointed off over the buildings.

The lights of the guard platforms were converging about three klicks away. "Something's going on at the Infirmary," Jack said.

The bot had its antennas out. "There's been an incident involving three groups of colonists."

"Stellar," Kit said. "We need the diversion. Let's move out."

Jack almost grinned. She sounded like one of those guys in a vid about the Euro-Asian War. "Move out," he muttered. She already had the wagon halfway down the street, the bot hovering just in front of her. He had to jog to catch up with them.

The plaza looked huge, lit by just a few lights on the edges, with no people rushing around. Jack helped Kit steer the wagon to the right lift door. He entered the code Annie had used. "We have to be quick," he said, "and we have to be quiet."

The bot whistled and spun its optics. "What's that?" it hissed.

"Where?" Kit's fingers dug into Jack's arm.

"Behind that planter." The probe shook.

Jack whipped around.

But it was just the Armstrong holo, waving a hand, talking away to the empty plaza.

"Sorry," the bot said. It buzzed softly. And said, "Sorry" again. "I thought it was Silver."

Jack freed the scooter from the wagon. Kit grabbed the handlebars, and he lifted the board, and together they lugged it into the lift. Jack went back for the suits and draped them over the scooter.

When the gees lightened, Kit stretched out her arms and did a slow spin. "Oh," she said, "I love this. Don't you love this?"

And Jack didn't even grab the sissy bar. Somehow, after tonight, zero gee felt . . . well, he didn't love it. But it felt almost normal.

As soon as the lift doors opened on the docking level, Jack poked out his head. A couple of strings of Perihelion beads, an empty glitter vial, and someone's coveralls floated in the corridor. But nothing else.

Jack's chest tightened, like the O-two level had just dropped. Silver finding them would be bad. But, all of a sudden, the thought of Annie finding them seemed a lot worse. He looked back at Kit and the bot. "It's the open door to our left," he whispered. "Hurry."

The scooter was floating in the middle of the lift. Kit gave it a shove. It flew out into the corridor and clanged against the wall. The two suits flopped loose.

"Oops," the bot said.

"Spam," Jack hissed. But no doors opened. No one came out to investigate. He glared at Kit. "I said, be quiet!" he whispered.

"I pushed too hard." Kit swam out of the lift. She grabbed the suits and stuffed them under her arm. She drifted around sideways. "Which way are we going?"

Jack grabbed the scooter's handlebars and maneuvered it down the corridor. Thank Calisto, the warehouse room was still open. He pushed the scooter inside. Dim lights came on automatically in all four corners. As soon as Kit and the bot were in, he closed the door. And took a good, deep breath.

The music from the next room pulsed and vibrated right through the wall. Something clattered and banged, and there was a loud burst of laughter.

"Wow," Kit said. "That must be some party."

"Must be," Jack said. He pointed to the far wall. "Air lock is over there." He pushed the scooter toward it. The bot was already opening the hatch.

As soon as they were all in, the bot sealed the hatch up tight. "Get into your suits," it said, hovering above the controls. "I'm going to drain the atmo."

The suit was like the one Jack had used for emergency evac drills. Just a few extra gauges and clamps. He had it on in less than five minutes. Kit still fumbled with the chest fasteners. "Didn't they teach you anything on the *Bradbury*?" He brushed her hands away and snapped the suit closed.

"We were in coach. They just showed us how to enter the pods." She tilted her head back so he could dog down the helmet.

Jack tapped the side. "You hear me okay? Comm working?"

She nodded. Her face was a little blurry behind the sun visor, but he could see her eyes, green as the bio readout glowing at the top of his own visor. She fiddled with her glove, and the tiny laser blade slid out from the tip of the index finger.

"Hey!" Jack flailed backward, just before the blade sliced right through his visor. "Watch it!"

"Sorry." Kit retracted the blade. "I was trying to tighten the wrist seal."

"Jupiter's eye." Jack grabbed her glove and adjusted the setting for her. "Leave the tools alone. Don't mess with anything else." She'd be a pancake without him. True fact.

"Three minutes to port opening," the bot said. Its voice was sharp and tinny in Jack's helmet. It was floating above the scooter's handlebars, two long manips plugged into the controls. An optic swiveled toward Kit and Jack. "You two ready?"

They both swam toward the scooter, collided in midair, and floated apart. "I get to drive," Kit said.

"No, you don't. You've never even been on a scooter before."

She flailed her arms, trying to swim around him. "How many times have you been on one?"

Jack reached out and just barely managed to snag the handlebars before she could. "Lots of times," he said. He swung his body into the front position, right behind the bot. Of course, he'd usually been the passenger, and Annie's dad had been driving. But Kit didn't need to know the details.

She snorted, like she suspected the details, but she settled into position behind him.

He glanced back. "You need help with your feet?"

"No," she snapped. "And Waldo's doing all the driving, you know. You're just standing there. It's not like you're doing anything special."

Jack grinned. He guided his own boots into the insets and made sure the mags gripped tight to the soles. His fingers felt sausage-fat and clumsy in the thick gloves. Careful not to jostle the bot, he rested his hands lightly on the handlebars next to the impulse controls.

"You need to slow your breathing, Jack," the bot said. "My readings show you're using air at an alarming rate."

"Ha," Kit said.

Jack tried to take steady, even breaths.

"The correct time," the bot said, "is 0007. Please keep your hands inside the scooter at all times." It buzzed.

"Waldo," Kit said. "This is serious."

It buzzed again. "The docking port will be open in three . . . two . . . one."

The whole outer hull fell away in front of them.

And the Black stretched out. As far as they could see. And farther.

"Glory," Kit said. Jack could feel her hands on his shoulders.

Jack let his breath out with a loud *whoosh*. It was always a surprise, no matter how many times you did it. It was always amazing.

The bot juiced the scooter, and they rode free of the station.

The sun was always surprising, too. So small and so far away, but still so bright. Even with his visor down, Jack had to squint his eyes.

"Welcome back the sun," the bot whispered.

"Welcome back the sun," Jack repeated. He turned his head away from the glare, and the frost-white stars shone around them. Clear, brittle light poking through the thick blackness all around them. In front of them and above them and below them. Like being in the chapel.

But nothing like the chapel. Nothing like it at all.

Jack took a deep, warming breath.

"Where is the Shipyard?" Kit's voice was a little high. A little tight. Like she had too much helium in her mix.

Jack pointed, and the scooter wobbled sideways under his feet, then corrected. "It looks like a star. See, that big one, blinking just north of Antares."

"Flash effort, Jack," the bot said. "And surprising for a human. Most of you can't orient so quickly." It sounded surprised.

"How long will it take to get there?" Kit asked.

"We'll continue at this rate of thrust for five more minutes. Then coast for nineteen minutes and forty-seven seconds. After the turnaround, we will thrust again."

"For another five minutes and fifteen seconds," Jack said.

"Stellar, Jack!" the bot said. And it sounded—Jack didn't know how it sounded. He didn't think anyone had ever talked to him like that before. Something fizzed inside him. Like he'd just bit down on a caff pill.

"Do you have a wafer up there or something?" Kit asked.

"I told you. I'm good with numbers." Jack looked back. The station was receding fast behind them.

The bot started to hum. And then to sing. "And Frankie found lo-o-ove."

Jack grinned. "And Frankie found lo-o-ove," he joined in.

"And Frankie found lo-o-ove," they sang together.

"On Plu-to," Jack finished, his voice cracking a little on the high note.

"Oh, please," Kit said, "shut off my air and compost me now."

Jack laughed. And the bot, suddenly floating free, bumped into his chest.

"Hey!" Jack let go of the handlebars and grabbed the bot. The probes, the optics, the antennas were all retracted. "Spam," Jack said.

"What? What's wrong?" Kit said.

He gave the bot a little shake. "Waldo?" No answer. "Waldo?" Jack shook him harder.

No answer. Not a quiver. Not a hum.

"What about Waldo?" Kit lurched sideways, leaning out, and the scooter lurched, too, slipping a little to the left.

"He's . . ." Jack took a deep breath. The air tasted sharp and metallic. "I think Waldo's dead."

TWELVE

"DEAD?" KIT'S voice made Jack's ears ring. "Waldo can't be dead. He's got his own reactor. He's going to run for thousands of years."

Jack stared down at the seamless blue surface. He tapped it gently. "Does he sleep then?"

"No, he doesn't sleep. Look. Give him to me." She tried to lean out and around. The scooter jerked sideways.

The mags held tight, but Jack still grabbed for the handlebars. "Stand still," he said. "Just stand really still." And then he saw that all the control dials were dark, too. "Spam."

"Just stop saying that!"

"There must have been a wave," Jack said. Drekking spit. He couldn't believe it. He couldn't believe he'd been so dim. "We didn't check the flare report." Checking for solar activity. That was the kind of thing bots were supposed to do. The kind of thing you relied on them to do.

"A wave?" He could tell Kit was looking around, like she was trying to see the ions flowing on by. "But we're okay." She didn't sound absolutely positive.

"These suits are state-of-the-art. All the tech is completely insulated," Jack said. And Fast Marco always put the most expensive ones at the front of the rack.

"So we're fine," Kit said. "And Waldo's got backup protocols. He just performed an emergency shutdown." Her teaching-vid voice and her diplomat voice rolled into one. All their problems solved.

"The thing is," Jack said, his voice very calm, "the scooter's tech is pranked too."

"What?" And Jack wished he could put his fingers in his ears. "You mean the computers aren't working?"

"Don't shout." Jack tapped one of the gauges. Nothing. "Obviously some of the deep internal stuff is working. The mags are working, or we wouldn't be standing here. The gyros must be working. And we've got juice." Jack could feel the vibration, up through the soles of his boots. So they were still accelerating. "Spam," he said.

Kit's hand bounced against the back of his helmet. "Stop saying that!"

"Suit. Chron display." Red numbers appeared on the top left side of Jack's visor, above his bio readout. "Kit. What did Waldo say? Before we left? What did he say the time was?"

"I don't . . . 0007? I think he said 0007."

The chron blinked 0013. Spam. Jack reached out and killed the juice. Like that would stop them.

Nothing stops you, in space. And no one can hear you whine.

"What did you do?" Kit was leaning forward again, peering around his arm.

"Turned off the juice." He tried to rub his head, but his glove just hit the side of his helmet. They'd miss the turnaround now. And if they missed the turnaround, they'd miss the Shipyard. They'd head straight on out beyond the satellite array.

They'd end up in their own orbit. A new little world. Kitandjack. Jackandkit. In their own orbit around the sun. Forever.

He glanced at his readout. Except they had air for only about two hours. So it would be a lifeless little world. Just the zip scooter, going around and around with two bodies stuck tight to the mags.

Kit hit him again, so hard this time his head rocked. "Don't you flatline, too, space boy." He heard her sigh. "Look. It's just numbers, Jack. That's all it is."

"What is?"

"Navigation. It's just numbers, and you're good at numbers, remember?"

He laughed. "I'm good at calculating the price of a special and a synale and a thirty percent tip. I'm good at figuring the markup on a vial of glitter. This"—he waved a hand at the tiny, frosty stars surrounding them—"this is different."

"It's not different. Not at all. It's still just numbers. You've got a chron, right? And you know our velocity."

Earthies always thought everything was so drekking simple. They couldn't understand how different everything was out here. "Right. So I can figure just how fast we're heading for Neptune. The problem, you kludge, is that we'll have to do a manual turnaround, at just the right second. And then I'll have to compute the juice back."

But, even as he said it, Jack realized he was starting to figure it, starting to run the numbers.

"So get us to the turnaround," Kit said, "and we'll work it out from there."

She sounded like Annie. And there was no sense arguing.

It took a long minute and a half for Jack to find Antares again, and then it took forty-seven even longer seconds to find the Yard and center it in the scope's target. All the while, Jack kept doing the computations over and over. Making absolutely sure he had them right.

He looked down at Waldo, still tight in the crook of his arm, and tried to remember what the bot had said to him. *Flash effort.* Not the words so much. But the way he had said them.

When the chron blinked to 0023, Jack took a deep breath. "Kit? You still back there?"

"Ha-ha."

"Okay, we have to get ready to do the manual turn-around."

"And what exactly does that mean? Do I get off and push or something?"

Jack almost smiled. "Kind of. We force the scooter to turn by changing our body position."

"Do you actually know how to do this?"

"Of course. I've done it before." Once. With Mitch. As a joke. *Let me show you how the old-timers did it, Jack.* And they'd been only about fifty meters from the station. "It's easy. True fact."

"What do we have to do?" Kit said.

Jack explained the procedure. And he wished he could see her face. Kit didn't say anything for twenty whole blinks of the chron. Then she sighed. "You'd better be right about this, Jack. This had better not be some kind of bizarre spacer joke."

"It's no joke. It'll work. Trust me." Jack slid open the pocket below his knee and stuffed Waldo inside. He didn't want to risk dropping him.

As the chron blinked over, he shouted, "Now!"

For one second, and then another, nothing happened. And then he felt the scooter start to shift. He didn't look back, but he knew Kit was windmilling her arms.

"Harder!" he shouted. "Faster!"

"I can't do this any faster!" she panted.

He rested his hand on the juice, bending into the scope. Just a little burst, on the cross axis. Just a nudge. A tickle.

The Yard disappeared from the target. Jack's heart made a sharp double beat. Stress warnings flashed on the bio readout. Monitors started to beep. His suit first. Then Kit's.

Slowly, slowly they were coming around.

"Stop!" Jack shouted. "Stop with the arms!" The Yard's light was back in the target. He hit the juice—one quick spurt—and checked the chron.

Kit gave a little half sob, half gasp. Her helmet pressed against his back. The monitors and stress warnings silenced.

"You okay?" Jack asked.

"Just tell me it worked. Tell me it drekking worked."

"It worked flash. You were cosmic." Jack watched the chron. And he counted off in his head, too. Just in case. Slowly, painfully slowly, the light in the center of the scope started to get bigger. And bigger.

"Jack!" The scooter wobbled. "Look!"

"I can't look. I'm watching the scope."

"No! Look!"

He lifted his head. And there it was. Right in front of them. Right where it should be. The Shipyard.

"You did it, Jack! You found it!" Kit's hands pounded, making his helmet vibrate.

Jack forced himself to let go of the sides of the scope. Forced himself to unclench his fingers in his gloves.

Not bad. Surprising even. For a human. He grinned. And he wished Waldo could have seen it.

"You know, it's funny," Kit said. Jack knew she had her head tilted the way she did. "It doesn't look exactly the way I remember it. I mean, when I was in Quarantine."

Jack looked up again. And it was the Shipyard, its own little universe, lights glowing on all its arms, illuminating the maintenance ports and the passenger arrival areas and the docking bays.

Only something was floating in between them and the Yard. Something big and black. Blocking out a large piece of it.

It faintly reflected the light from the Shipyard. Like a shadow satellite. A hodgepodge of ships welded together. Transports, skiffs, even a few escape pods. The blackened hull of a freighter jutted out from the middle.

Jack had to cough the words out. "We're on the wrong side."

"What do you mean, the wrong side?"

He leaned back. Back and away. Trying to push the scooter back and away. They just kept right on coasting forward.

"That's the Junkyard," Jack said. All of a sudden, he felt really, really cold. Like the Black itself had found a way inside his suit. Inside his skin. But it hadn't, of course. He checked his readout. Everything was still sealed up tight.

And he started trying to figure. If they eased over on the cross axis. And he timed a burst of juice. But he couldn't make the numbers fall into place. They were frozen somewhere in the back of his brain.

"Uh-oh," Kit said. "Who are those guys?"

Three figures were silhouetted against the dark bulk of the freighter. The exhaust from their packs lighting up the darkness behind them.

"Junkies," Jack said.

"Well, spam," Kit said.

There was nothing they could do. The junkies were within grappling range in just a few minutes. All three of them looked big and thick. It was just the suits, Jack reminded himself. They all wore mismatched suits and helmets, spare pieces from different sets. Inside they were just . . . junkies.

The scooter rocked as the grappler bot smacked silently into the chassis, just below Jack's left foot. Immediately the bot started crab-walking up toward the handlebars and the controls. Jack moved his hands out of the way.

Kit sucked in her breath, but she didn't say anything.

The biggest junkie floated up beside Jack. "You kids out having a little Perihelion fun?" Female, Jack could tell from her voice. The sun shield obscured her face. Gloved hands grabbed the handlebars.

"We got caught in that radiation wave," Jack said. "Pranked out the tech. So, Pluto! We're really glad to see you." He knew she couldn't see his smile. But he tried for one anyway.

The scooter shook. One of the other junkies had grabbed the back. The third junkie was floating about thirty meters away, hanging on to the end of the grappler's tether.

"I say strip 'em, Liv. Strip 'em here. Take the scooter and the suits," said the one back by Kit.

The junkie near Jack turned her head. "Leave 'em to drift, you think, Zeph?"

"Drek! Drek!" It was the third junkie. "I've sprung a leak!"

They all turned to look. He had let go of the tether, and it snaked up and around him. He had a hand clamped to the shoulder joint of his suit. "I'm losing pressure!" His voice was panicky.

Jack could see the force of the escaping air, pushing him back and away.

"Too bad, Dougie." Liv knocked the grappling bot free of the handlebars. "Come on, Zeph. Let's take 'em on in."

The second junkie moved up to the other side, wedging

Jack between him and Liv. They fired their packs, and the change in gees pushed Jack back against Kit.

"You can't leave me out here!" Dougie screamed. "Come on! Guys! I've got credit! I'll pay you!"

"Ah, you'll pancake before you know it," Liv said. And Zeph laughed.

"Wait! Wait! Guys? Bastards!"

His screams didn't cut off until they were out of comm range.

Jack forced himself to keep staring straight ahead.

THIRTEEN

THE JUNKIES glided Jack and Kit through the open port in the freighter hull. Smooth and cool as a kelp latte.

The port closed behind them. And it was pitch-dark.

Jack felt Kit bump against him. He heard her take a deep, shuddering breath. "I can't believe—"

"Shut up!" Zeph said.

"But you can go back. He's probably still alive. It actually takes—"

"Shut up!" Zeph and Liv both shouted.

There was complete silence for a minute and forty-eight seconds by Jack's chron. And then he heard the faint chime of an atmo meter.

A door opened in the back wall, and the two junkies pushed the scooter through.

Lights sputtered on as soon as the door closed. Must have some kind of private generator. Jack flipped up his sun shield and looked around.

The freighter had probably been old before it was junked. Now it was really old. Jack realized he was looking up at the floor, at the flat tops of workstations. They were in some kind of tech lab. Storage cupboards and lockers lined three walls.

Zeph released the mags, and Jack and Kit both floated

free of the scooter. "Welcome to the freighter *Jules Verne*," Zeph said. He shoved them both out of the way.

Jack bounced against the wall. And saw his own reflection. It was a plexy window. A cargo bay stretched out on the other side, big as the pub. He started to float back toward Zeph, but he caught the top edge of a cupboard and stopped himself.

Kit had bounced, too, but she flipped herself back around and faced the junkies. "What kind of people are you?" she demanded. "To just leave somebody to die like that?"

Liv was unclasping her helmet. "It was Dougie or Dougie's share of the credit." She pulled off her helmet and a cloud of long, frizzy dark hair surrounded her face.

She was, maybe, half an orbit older than Jack. And she reminded him . . . he couldn't think who she reminded him of.

She glared at him. "What are you staring at, kid?"

He shook his head. "Nothing."

Zeph had pulled off his helmet, too. He was about Liv's age, his hair done up in fat dreads. "And Dougie's credit is worth way more than Dougie."

"I thought junkies were old," Kit said.

"Yeah, well, don't believe everything they tell you in Nursery," Liv said. And she laughed, a sharp crow of a laugh.

Jack started to undo his helmet. "Not you!" Liv said. "You use up your own air. Not ours." She bent her head toward Zeph and said something. Their voices were muffled by the helmets. But Jack caught, "Let 'em know we found them."

And it was like a big hand had reached out and closed

off his air valve. "You were waiting for us, weren't you?"

"They were what?" Kit said. She looked back at the junkies. "They're working for Silver?"

Jack thought they were going to deny it. But then Liv grinned, her even teeth glinting in the dim lights. "She sent us a bounce. She'd intercepted a report of an air lock being opened. Figured you were off-station. We came out our front door, and there you were. I guess that solar wave blew you right to us."

"Couldn't believe our luck," Zeph said.

Jack pressed his hand over Waldo, still safely closed up in his pocket. They'd come all this way from the station. They'd figured the course. They'd done the drekking manual turn-around. Just to get caught by Silver's partners? Zeph was wrong. Gert was right. There was no luck in the Black.

"While we wait, I'm stripping that scooter," Zeph said. He pulled himself up to one of the workstations.

"Be glad we're the ones who found you." Liv was bending over the scooter's control panel, prying it up. "We're not the only ones in this freighter. And some people are not as nice as we are."

"Not as nice at all," Zeph said, swimming down with a laser driver in each hand.

The two of them started ripping out the scooter's tech.

There had to be something they could do. But Jack's brain had clenched up again. His own emergency shut-down. He couldn't get a thought out.

Kit grabbed his arm and jerked him around. She peered into his helmet. Her eyes were huge, and her eyebrows waggled up and down. She mouthed something, something Jack couldn't hear. And she pointed toward the plexy, her eyes getting even bigger.

She was going to use up all her air, flailing around like that. "Don't panic," Jack said. He put a hand on her arm and leaned closer, his helmet resting against hers. "We'll work it out," he whispered. And he hoped he sounded like he believed it.

Kit gave a strangled little shriek. Then she shoved back around him and swam over to the plexy. Like she couldn't stand to look at him anymore.

Jack put his hand over Waldo again. Think. There had to be a way. There had to be something. They were in a tech lab. And a tech lab should have a bot dock, should have some way to reboot Waldo. Jack craned his neck to look up toward the workstations. If they could get Waldo running, he could help. He could think of something.

Zeph muttered. And Liv laughed again, that same crowing laugh. She had pulled her hair back and fastened it with a piece of loose wire.

And Jack remembered. He turned back toward them. "I know you," he said.

Zeph groaned. "I can gag him," he said, not looking up.

"Get that gyro out first," Liv said.

"No, really." Jack tried to snap his fingers, but the gloves were too thick. "You're Rigel's sister."

Liv's head came up. She was holding the scooter's scope in her hand. She was frowning.

Jack held on to the top of the cupboard. "You are. Rigel's sister. You worked for Ollie. You got into a fight one day. With a geek. You dumped his order of squid noodles over his head." It had been funny. At the time.

Liv and Zeph were both staring at him. "Your name was Cass then," Jack added. And he was glad for the helmet obscuring some of his face. Because he'd never told anybody, certainly not Rigel—but he'd sort of liked her. Rigel's sister. Especially after the noodle thing.

Jack thought about Dougie. And pushed the thought away.

"Yeah, well, I changed my name," Liv snapped. "I changed a lot of things."

"But you worked in food service?" Zeph was looking at her, a funny kind of shocked look on his face.

"Why do you think I left? Like I was going to spend the rest of my life serving mechs and geeks and all the other waste products of Freedom Station." Liv pointed the laser driver at Jack. "And don't start thinking we've got some kind of history, kid. Because I don't remember you at all."

Jack glanced over at Kit. She was still floating tight by the plexy, one hand extended toward it. Like she was reaching out for the other side. And he wanted to tell her he had an idea. He wanted to tell her that they were maybe going to need some diplomat skills. But she didn't turn around.

"Food service," Zeph said again.

"Shut up," Liv said.

Jack turned back to them. He cleared his throat. "Rigel said you'd gotten a place on Independence Station. He said something better opened up, and the Company had moved you out there."

The scope was floating next to her arm. Liv batted it, and it went spinning halfway across the room. "Is that what they're telling everybody? What a family." And she said it like she was spitting out scum.

Jack looked around the room. Slowly. The corrosion on the ceiling below him. The broken edges of a fan sticking out from its housing. The dirt particles floating in the corners. The ragged pair of inners and the bag of nutricubes hooked to a locker door. He was glad he had the helmet on, glad he didn't have to smell the atmo. "I guess things out here are just a lot better. I mean, than living on a station."

"You bet they are." Liv was using the laser driver on a pressure gauge. "No rules. No regs. No Company telling you when to eat, when to sleep, when to use the head."

"Only way to live," Zeph said.

"No one loves the Company. That's a true fact," Jack said. He cleared his throat. If he had believed it, he could convince them, too. "You ever wonder how come Silver knows everything she knows? Like who's leaving the station?"

They both looked up. "What are you talking about?" Liv said.

Jack shrugged. "Seems to me only someone with

Company connections could do something like that."

"Are you saying Silver's working for the Company?" Zeph said.

"*Yes!*" Kit shouted.

They all looked.

"Jack!" She was pointing toward the plexy. She'd cut a hole right in the middle with her suit's laser blade. "This way!" And she pulled herself through the hole, with about a centimeter to spare on each side.

"Hey!" Zeph shouted. And Liv hauled herself around the scooter.

Jack treaded air. Then his fingers caught the edge of the cupboard again.

"Stop!" Liv shouted.

Jack pushed himself forward as hard as he could. The angle was bad. The hole seemed to grow smaller and smaller the closer he got. He closed his eyes. He felt a hitch, a tug. But no suit monitors went off.

He opened his eyes, and he was out in the cargo bay.

Kit grabbed him before he could spin off too far. "This way!" She started pulling herself along the wall, heading for a big door off to their left, towing Jack behind her.

Jack wiggled free and reached for the wall himself. Hand over hand, he pulled himself along. Faintly, he heard Zeph shout, "It's too small! I won't fit."

He and Liv would have to go through the tech lab door.

"Faster!" Jack shouted to Kit. "Faster!"

Her head bobbed, her feet flapped, and she speeded up.

Jack hauled himself after her. At any second, he knew he'd feel hands grabbing his feet. Knew he'd hear Liv shout, "Got you!"

"Don't be locked. Don't be locked. Don't be locked." It took him a second to realize it was Kit's panicky whispers and not his own thoughts.

She had stopped at the panel. She slapped the control. "Don't be locked." And the big door opened.

They both swam out into the main corridor of the freighter. Jack found the panel on the opposite side. As the door slid back across, he saw Zeph and Liv, swimming out of the tech lab.

The door clanged shut.

The corridor was dark, barely lit by faint red emergency lights set into the floor above them.

"This way," Kit hissed. "This way." She headed down the corridor to the right.

"Wait!"

"Shut up and swim," she said.

Jack flailed out with his right hand and pulled himself along after her.

She came to another corridor and turned down it. "Crew quarters are this way."

Why in the name of Phobos was she looking for the crew quarters? "We need to find another air lock." Behind him, Jack caught a flash of light. The door to the cargo bay opening. He pulled faster after Kit.

She was already halfway down the corridor. There were closed doors on each side. And Jack remembered what Liv had said. *We're not the only ones in this freighter.* He pulled after Kit. "Wait. Wait."

She stopped, suddenly. "In here." She swam through an open door.

Jack peered inside. It was dark. Too dark to see anything. "Kit. Another junkie may live here."

"Then he shouldn't leave his drekking door open," Kit whispered back. She spun in midair. "We gotta find a place to hide. They'll be right behind us."

Jack shifted, and the light from outside lit a small patch of the room. "There's a bunk. On the ceiling. I mean, up there on the floor."

"Flash! We'll hide under the bed!"

Kit swam across, grabbed the frame of the bunk, pulled herself up and wedged herself between the bottom of the bunk and the floor.

Jack pulled himself up flat beside her. The bottom of the bunk made an edge just high enough for him to duck behind.

Almost immediately, the narrow beam of a handheld light lit up the corridor outside. Jack held his breath.

The light slid into the room. Across the middle. Into the corners. And then down. Whoever was holding it was a dark shape hanging on to the door frame.

Zeph.

The light came up and slid across the bunk. But not up high enough.

The light flowed past, over the wall, and then back out the door. And Zeph swam after it.

Jack heard the sputter of Kit's breath. "Okay," she said. "Let's go." She pushed at him.

"Wait. This is a Sirocco-class freighter. They're huge. We could be blundering around for days. We've got to stop. We've got to think."

"I know it's a Sirocco-class. I had to build a model of one for my History of Transportation exam." She pushed at him again.

"History of—"

"Never mind." She shoved, and he was out from under the bunk, floating free in the room. And she was floating beside him. "I know where there's another air lock. Just aft of the navigation room." She grabbed the door frame. "If we can get to the air lock, we can get out of here. Before Silver gets here."

And Kit swam out into the corridor.

She headed left. The same way Zeph had gone. "They've split up," Jack said, following her. "Liv could be anywhere. And Zeph might come back this way."

"Shh. I'm counting." About forty meters down the corridor, she said, "Here." She slid open a panel. "It's a wiring access tunnel," Kit said. "It connects to the ship's main corridor."

Jack followed her feet through the opening. "How detailed was this drekking model you made?"

"I got the highest grade on the exam."

Jack's shoulders brushed against both sides of the tunnel. He had to wiggle his hands up so he could use them to push along.

He hoped no junkies had decided a wiring access tunnel would be the perfect place to make a nest.

"Five minutes," Kit said. "We'll be out in less than five minutes." She sounded a little breathless. Like she'd been thinking about junkies, too.

"But what do we do once we're out? Have you thought about that?" Jack asked.

She stopped, and Jack's helmet rammed right into her boots. "I'm just getting us out of here," she snapped. "You can figure out how to get us to the Shipyard." And she started forward again.

"Oh, stellar." Jack checked his bio readout. Still fifty-eight minutes of air left. Depending on where they came out of the Junkyard, it might be possible to work their way over to the Shipyard. He started calculating.

"Oof!" He ran into Kit's feet again.

"We're here," she hissed. "And the panel's already open."

Slowly they swam out into the corridor. There were no emergency lights here. Even though there was no grav, even though nothing weighed anything, Jack felt like the darkness was squishing down on him, trying to flatten him. But he didn't dare turn on his helmet light.

Something grabbed his sleeve. "Drek!"

"It's me, space boy. This way. We go past the captain's

quarters and another tech lab." She was reciting the doors as they pulled past them.

Jack held his breath, hoping none of the doors opened. Hoping no junkies came swimming out.

"The communications room," Kit whispered.

The door slid open. Light poured out of the room. Blinding them.

Jack's hands scrabbled for purchase on the wall. Kit thrashed backward, her arms and legs waving and kicking.

A black shadow loomed in the doorway, cutting off the light. "What in the name of Phobos—"

Jack managed to catch himself on the edge of the door. "Holy living spam," he said.

"Jack?" the shadow said.

"Booker John?" Jack said.

"Who?" Kit said.

"Hey!" Liv shouted.

Jack and Kit and Booker John all turned to look.

Zeph and Liv were at the far end of the corridor. Pulling along the wall. Coming fast.

"We found them!" Zeph shouted.

"This way." Booker John pushed off and shot down the corridor.

Kit grabbed the wall and pushed off after him.

Jack followed them. His helmet filled with a roaring, his own breathing and heartbeat, so loud it drowned out everything else.

Booker John pulled to a stop and opened a door. The other air lock. The outer hatch was already gaping open. There was nothing outside but the Black.

Jack and Kit were sucked in after Booker John. He hit the switch to close and seal the door.

Warning klaxons blared as someone tried to override the door code.

Jack checked his pocket. Waldo was still there.

"Jump!" Booker John shouted.

FOURTEEN

"JUMP!" BOOKER John shouted again.

"Stop!" Liv was pounding on the inner door.

Jack grabbed the edge of the open hatch and peered out. And then he saw it. Drifting on its mooring cable two hundred meters away. A Mistral-class transport.

"We made a—" Zeph howled.

And Jack didn't know if he jumped or if Booker John pushed him, but all of a sudden, he was out of the freighter, and the stars were flowing past all around him.

"Aim for the handholds!" Booker John's voice echoed in his helmet.

"What drekking handholds?" Jack yelled. The transport was rising in front of him. Expanding. And then he could see them. A whole series of handholds surrounding the air lock hatch.

He stuck out both hands. Not thinking about what would happen if he missed the grab. Not thinking about bouncing off the side. Spinning free. Sailing off somewhere to orbit out past the Oort cloud.

Jack hit the side of the ship. His left glove brushed something, started to slide off. He clamped his fingers down, hard and fast.

And he stopped. He was dangling from the handhold, his body floating out behind him.

"Drek!" Kit screamed. And she hit and clung just below Jack.

And then Booker John was there. Grabbing a handhold on the other side of the hatch and entering a code into the panel all in one move.

The hatch opened. Booker John and Kit swung inside. Jack looked back at the Junkyard. He could see the open port on the freighter. But no sign of Liv and Zeph. He swam into the air lock.

Booker John sealed the hatch.

Kit had wedged herself into a corner. She floated, hunched over, head down, her arms and legs splayed out.

"Are you okay?" Jack asked.

Her helmet swung from side to side. No. And then up and down. Yes.

Jack took it as a maybe.

The atmo meter chimed. "Welcome aboard the transport ship *Larry Niven*," it said.

Booker John was already undoing his helmet. Jack hauled off his gloves and started unfastening his suit. But Kit had hers off first.

She pulled off her helmet and shook out her hair, dripping wet. She took a deep breath. And then another. Her coverall was dark with sweat. She rubbed her hands, hard, over her face, through her hair. "That was . . . at the end there . . ." She shook her head.

Booker John had his suit off and was folding it into a locker. He had on a black flight suit with no insignia patches. "A little too close to 'Exit pursued by a bear.'" He nodded toward Kit. "I don't think we've been introduced."

"This is Kit," Jack said. "She's the—" He nearly said "rat" and stopped. "She's the one I said I saw going over the fence. Remember? Back at the pub."

"Ah, yes. Back at the pub," Booker John said. A small, tight smile creased his lips.

"But this was so lucky," Kit said. She was grinning. "When that door opened, I thought we were debris for sure. I thought you were going to be another junkie."

"It was lucky," Booker John said. And now he really smiled. Relaxed and easy. All his face lifting. "I can't quite believe it myself."

Jack had his suit off. He checked the pocket one more time, felt Waldo's reassuring solidity. "They can't come after us." Jack nodded toward the hatch. "Zeph and Liv. Can they?"

"One thing I've learned," Booker John said, "is never underestimate junkies. We'd better put some distance between us and them." He opened the door to the inside of the ship. "I suggest you make yourselves comfortable in the galley. We'll have to pull some gees for a little bit."

He went out into the corridor. Jack and Kit swam after him.

"Wait!" Kit grabbed his arm. She took a deep breath, like she was about to leap into a ponic tank. "I need a job. I need you to hire me."

Booker John's eyes bugged, just a little. Jack wondered if he'd ever seen Booker John surprised before. By anything. And then the actor threw back his head and laughed. "Now that," he said, shaking his head, chuckling, "that was the absolute last thing I was expecting you to say."

"I've got the skills," Kit said. "And I played Puck. Back on Earth. In school."

Booker John looked at Jack, his eyebrows arched.

"I don't know about the puck stuff, but she's loaded with skills," Jack said. "True fact."

"Well," Booker John said. He pushed at the loose hairs floating free from his braid. "Let's discuss it when we're sure we're out of the junkies' range."

"Okay," Kit said. "Okay. We'll talk about it then."

Jack looked up and down the corridor. It was empty. And the doors, opening up at regular intervals on each side, were dark. It was so quiet, he could hear the hush-hush of the atmo scrubbers. "Are we the only ones on board?"

Booker John nodded. "I had the ship in for repairs. I'm meeting up with the rest of the crew at the South Dock in a few hours."

"You can pilot the ship by yourself?" And it sounded . . . Jack shrugged. "I didn't know you had pilot training."

Booker John grinned. "You'd be amazed what you can learn when you have to, Jack." He pointed down the corridor. "The galley's three doors that way. Bins are fully stocked. Help yourselves to the nutricubes." And he pulled himself in the opposite direction down the corridor and then up a passageway in the ceiling.

As soon as his feet disappeared, Kit whipped around. She

was grinning, the widest, happiest grin Jack had ever seen on her. "This is stellar, Jack! This is working out perfectly!"

"He hasn't hired you yet."

"But he will. I know he will. He likes me. I can tell." She pointed at the suit Jack was still clutching. "Let's get Waldo rebooted. I want to find a good place to hide him now, before the rest of the crew comes on board."

"We'll have to find the tech lab." Jack opened up the pocket and pulled out Waldo. "I don't suppose you made a model of a Mistral-class."

"I got the highest grade for that one, too." She grabbed Waldo and started pulling herself down the corridor with her free hand.

Jack shoved the suit back into the air lock and followed her.

The ship was designed for deep-space travel. There were handholds spaced out along the walls, to make it easier to move in zero gee. All the walls and the floor and the ceiling were covered in soft, nubby carpeting. So "up" and "down" made no difference. Everything was the same. They passed the head, the galley, crew quarters. The whole place smelled of cleanser and the disinfectant that scrubber bots used on tough stains. The smell reminded Jack of the pub just before a health inspection. It smelled good.

The last door at the end of the corridor opened on a cargo bay. "This way," Kit said.

The bay was much smaller than the one on the freighter. The tech lab was halfway down the left-hand wall.

As Kit opened the door, Jack felt just the faintest tug of grav. "Attitude thrusters," he said. "To maneuver away from the Junkyard."

"Flash," she said. And she swam into the tech lab.

It was smaller than the one on the freighter, too. But it was right-side up. Long tables, divided into workstations, and lockers and storage cupboards covered all the walls. There was no plexy window into the cargo bay. A hatch on the back wall was labeled ESCAPE POD. So the mechs and the geeks wouldn't have to go down with the ship.

The bot dock was set into the workstation right next to the door. Kit positioned Waldo over the inset, and the mags sucked him in and held him tight. "A reboot shouldn't take more than—"

"A few seconds," Waldo finished.

The mags released, and he flew up out of the dock. His optics, antennas, and manips all extended. His antennas shuddered. "That was very unpleasant. Like a data overload on top of a systems malfunction."

"Serves you right," Kit said.

"But you're okay now?" Jack asked.

"I'm fine." And Waldo sounded embarrassed. "I should have checked that flare report. I got a little excited, I guess."

Kit rolled her eyes, but Jack laughed. Because he completely understood.

Waldo was scanning the room. "What happened after I shut down?"

"I had to drive the scooter," Jack said. "I deadsticked it in," he added. Not wanting to make a big deal out of it.

"Jack!" Waldo flew up in front of him, buzzing loudly. "That's cosmic!" He looked at Kit. "Isn't that cosmic?"

"Oh, yeah. You should have seen how cosmic it was when we ended up at the Junkyard."

"Anybody could have made that mistake," Jack said.

"But we're not in the Junkyard now." Waldo was flying around the room, checking things out closer. He opened a locker.

About thirty maintenance bots floated inside. Their optics and antennas extended. "Is there a maintenance problem?" they all asked in their tinny little voices.

Waldo buzzed.

And very faintly, almost like an echo, Jack heard a ping from the comm by the door. The sound of a bounce coming into a communications grid. Someone contacting the ship.

"You won't believe how perfect this is, Waldo." Kit had pulled over next to him. "This is Booker John's ship. We just found him. Right there in the Junkyard. And he's going to hire me on. He's going to take us to Seattle Prime."

Waldo's optics flicked toward Jack.

"There's a good chance," Jack said.

And there must have been something in his voice. Because Kit looked at him, too. A funny, pained look on her face. "Oh, Jack. You can't take the scooter back to Fast Marco." She frowned. "They aren't going to blame you, are they? I mean, they won't know you helped us?"

Waldo gave a soft click.

"No, they won't know." Jack shrugged. "I'll get Booker John to drop me off at the South Dock. I'll be back in the pub before Gert, most likely."

"Oh. That's okay then." But she still had that funny look. "So you'll just go back to normal."

"Right." Normal. "Until I go out to Liberty."

"Liberty?" Her head tilted. And Waldo clicked again.

"I'm transferring out there. I've got a new job out there. And some family, maybe." And, for the first time, he didn't grin when he said it. "I guess I never mentioned it."

She nodded. "Well, we didn't have a lot of time. To mention a lot of things."

"Everything okay back there?" Booker John's voice boomed out, so sudden and so loud, all three of them jumped and wobbled in midair. "Find those nutricubes okay?"

Jack pushed the comm reply button next to the door. "Uh. Everything's flash, Booker John. We found everything we need."

Kit muffled a laugh, and Waldo gave a soft buzz.

"Stellar," Booker John said. "But now I need the two of you to strap in."

"Strap in?" Jack repeated.

"That's right. I'm going to hit the juice. We've got some unwanted company."

FIFTEEN

WALDO AND Kit had moved closer. Jack looked at them. They both shrugged. "Company?" he said into the comm.

"Is it Liv and Zeph?" Kit asked.

"Gees increase in thirty-five seconds," Booker John said.

Waldo clunked back into the dock. Jack grabbed the seat at the nearest workstation. Kit strapped in across from him. The drive started to whine just as Jack fastened the last buckle on his webbing.

And the weight hit. Jack sucked in air as the force pushed him back. He knew they had to be pulling less than a gee, but it felt like a giant hand trying to press him through the seat, across the room, through the wall, and right on out the hull. He could feel the skin on his face, pulling back tight against his skull.

He tried to count off the seconds, tried to figure how fast, how long, how far.

He could see Kit, her head hard against the headrest. Her lips pulled back in a big, smiley grimace.

And then the force was gone.

Jack choked in air, gingerly reinflating his lungs. He unfastened his straps and floated free. He felt less than weightless. Like he hardly existed at all.

Kit was up out of her seat, too. "Where are we going? Back to the station?"

Jack shook his head. Even though he had no weight, something very heavy sat right in the middle of his chest. "Burn was too long." They had to be at least a hundred klicks away from the station.

Waldo came up out of the dock. Both his antennas were extended. "We're now 398 klicks beyond Freedom Station in the direction of Tau Ceti."

"Three hundred ninety-eight klicks?" Kit said.

"Tau Ceti?" Jack said. Waldo's optics swung toward him, and they exchanged a look. What the drek was in that direction?

Jack swam over and keyed the comm call button. "Booker John?"

There was no answer.

Kit pushed over to the door and hit the switch. The door didn't open. She punched the switch. "Open up!" she shouted. "Right now!"

"Is it stuck?" Jack shoved her aside and hit the switch, too. Nothing happened.

"I did that already!" Kit shouted.

"Well, it doesn't hurt to try it again!" Jack shouted back.

"And yelling doesn't help." Waldo flew over and hooked up to the panel. He sighed. "It's been encrypted. I can break it. But it will take a while."

"What is going on?" Kit glared at Jack. Like he would know. "Where's Booker John taking us?"

Jack tried the comm again. "Booker John," he said, "we're in the tech lab. Not the galley." He'd think up a good excuse. Later. "And the door is pranked. We can't get out."

For a second, there was nothing but the hollow static of an empty grid. Then Booker John said, "Brace yourselves."

The ship rocked, violently, from side to side.

Jack banged up against the wall. Kit was knocked sideways into one of the workstations. She grabbed the edge to keep from sailing halfway across the room. "What was that?"

"Pulse torpedo," Waldo said. His right antenna was tilted up and out. "We've been intercepted by another ship. Grapplers and mooring cables and a portable air lock have been deployed."

Kit's face was whiter than her hair. "Is it the Company?"

"They haven't identified themselves." Waldo's optics twitched. "But it is a Typhoon-class." He looked at Jack.

Jack closed his eyes, opened them. "Fastest ship made," he said. Even though Kit had probably built a drekking model. "Some are privately owned. The Company uses them for search and rescue. Search and—"

"Capture," Waldo finished.

Kit groaned.

"Booker John did his best," Jack said. Because he had to say something. "But a transport's not designed for speed. There's no way the *Niven* could outrun a Typhoon."

Waldo spun in midair, his optics and probes and antennas all scanning. "We have to get off this ship. Before the boarding party arrives."

"The drekking door is locked!" Kit shouted. "We can't even get out of this drekking room!"

Waldo flew over to the escape pod access. "Then we'll go out another way." He tweaked the controls, and the access door opened.

Kit and Jack swam over, too. They all looked into the garage.

The pod hung floating near the outer hatch. It didn't look much bigger than Jack's room back behind the pub.

Kit frowned. "What's the range on one of these?"

"Back to the station, easy," Jack said. "It'll take a while."

"I'll modify the drive," Waldo said. "Get in." He pushed at them with his probes.

Kit's eyes glinted. "Maybe it could take us all the way to Seattle Prime."

"Oh, sure," Jack said. "If Waldo can modify the fabric of space, too."

"Just get in the drekking pod!" Waldo shouted.

The tech lab door started to slide open.

Waldo zipped out of sight under one of the workstations.

"I promise you." Booker John floated in the doorway. He looked at Jack and Kit. Apologetically, Jack thought. "I was not attempting to get away with anything." He swam into the tech lab.

"I know what you were attempting." Jack would recognize the voice anywhere. Silver swam in behind Booker John. She was holding a stun rod to the side of his neck.

Jack swung back so hard and so fast, he bumped against the wall. Kit gave a little half yelp, half gasp.

Silver ignored them. Her head was bare. Her electrodes

winked in the lights. "Liv and Zeph pinged me from the *Verne*. Said you'd jumped with the kids. Just after I'd talked to you. Just after I told you they had the bot. And as soon as I pinged you here on the *Niven*, you hit the juice." Silver shoved Booker John, hard enough to send him spinning across the room and to push herself back. "I can't believe you thought this ship could outrun the *Le Guin*, you double-crossing piece of scum."

Kit was hanging on to the doorway of the pod garage. "Why would you tell Booker John we had Waldo?"

"Who?" Silver said.

Jack caught a blur, out of the corner of his eye, but when he looked, Waldo had disappeared again.

Booker John pushed himself off the wall and straightened up. "I would never double-cross a partner, Silver," he said.

"Partner?" Kit said. Her voice was getting louder and sharper with each word.

Jack's mouth was trying to hang open. He snapped it shut. "You're working with Silver?" And he knew he sounded like he was still in Nursery. But he couldn't help it.

"Purely a business arrangement, believe me," Booker John snapped. And for a second, he looked like the play guy again. The Macbeth guy.

Silver was staring at Kit. "Did you steal that baggage from the *Bradbury*, kid?" She shook her head. "Drekking rats."

Booker John laughed, a dry, flat laugh. "Why is it that we never seem to learn that we shouldn't judge a book by its cover?" He made a wide, sweeping gesture toward Kit. "Allow me to introduce Jack's Earthie friend. Abner Kennedy Boston's only daughter, Katherine."

Katherine? Jack looked at her, but Kit was glaring at Booker John.

"She's Abner's kid?" Silver's amber eyes widened. "True fact?"

"Oh, yes," Booker John said when Kit didn't answer. "I accessed a copy of the *Bradbury*'s manifest in the comm room of the *Verne*. She was listed as tech support." Booker John chuckled. "I guess your friend Abner had a sense of humor."

"He never even mentioned he had a kid." Silver slid her stun rod into the holster on her boot. "Not in all the messages we exchanged." She almost sounded hurt.

Kit swam closer. The room seemed even smaller now, with all of them in there. "You were exchanging messages with my father?"

Across the room, Jack saw Booker John bend down, looking under the workstation.

Silver jerked a thumb toward her chest. "He was coming out to Seattle Prime to meet me, kid."

"No, he wasn't!" And now Kit sounded truly shocked. "He was going to meet some geeks. He was going to meet other people who were doing research on artificial intelligence."

Silver was grinning. "That was me," she said. "That was me, all along. And when I heard he'd been composted, I came on in. To collect my bot." Her grin widened, stretching her skin tight across her face. "I promised your father I'd give that bot a nice, safe home with a whole bunch of other smart bots."

"You're the geek from Seattle Prime?" Jack said.

Kit's frown lifted, her whole face brightening. "You're going to take Waldo back to the other geeks on Seattle Prime?"

"That's just what I told your father. So he'd agree to the deal." Silver shook her head, like she couldn't believe she had to explain this. "And who the drek is this Waldo?" She looked around the room.

"Oh," Booker John said, "you can't tell the players without a program." He was opening a locker. "Don't you get it, Silver? This maintenance bot has a name."

"A name? A bot doesn't need a name." Silver shook her head. "Well, it doesn't matter if you call it 'Granny.' I'm not taking that bot to Seattle Prime. I'm taking it to Pallas. To upgrade our defense and defend the colony."

And Jack remembered what she'd said back in the pub. *A colony desperate for defense.*

"Waldo doesn't know anything about defense," Kit said.

"What the bot knows isn't important," Silver said. "What's important are the prototypes and the augments."

The heaviness in Jack's chest tightened. He couldn't look at Kit. He had been wrong about Booker John. But Kit, Kit and her father, they had been wrong about everything.

Booker John slid open a drawer under the workstation.

"We need the bot's processors," Silver said. "so we can develop better weapons."

"What do you mean, 'we can develop better weapons?'" Jack asked. "Who's we?"

Silver smiled. "We are the people of the Pallas colony. And we have intelligence reports that show that New Oslo, in alliance with Perseverance, is stockpiling weapons of mass destruction. We have to increase our own weapons inventory. To prepare to defend ourselves. To maintain our unique presence in the solar system. To maintain a balance in the Black."

"You," Kit said, "are seriously dysfunctional."

Booker John laughed and opened another locker.

"Wait a minute." Jack pushed himself closer to Silver. "You're working for the Earthies on Pallas? You're helping some rusty Earth colony?" He saw Silver's smile widen. Spam. "You're telling me you're an Earthie?"

Silver tapped her electrodes. "Like the man said, kid. You can't always judge by the external looks."

Jack watched Booker John open a cupboard near the door. "But you're a spacer, right?" Jack said. "Booker John, I know you're a spacer." Although he didn't. He didn't know anything anymore.

Booker John glanced back. "Oh, I'm a spacer. Flesh and blood."

"So why are you helping her? Why are you helping Pallas?"

Booker John closed the cupboard and opened the storage

bin next to the bot dock. "Acting doesn't quite pay my bills, and I have to supplement my income any way I can. As I said, this is strictly a business proposition for me." He put his hand over his heart. "It's the credit I care about, Jack. Not the cause. True fact. And Silver here has promised me that we're talking about a great deal of credit."

"But Waldo doesn't know anything about defense," Kit said again. Like they were all missing the important point here. The vital fact. "Waldo's not a weapon. He would never hurt anyone. He wouldn't want to hurt anyone."

Silver laughed. "Bots don't want anything. And this bot contains prototypes for augmented processors. Processors we need."

"But he's sentient!" Kit shouted. Her eyes were very big and very shiny. "He's not just prototypes and processors and enhanced memory!"

Booker John spun slowly to look at her.

"So it's true?" Silver frowned. "Your father wasn't just spouting spam? It's really self-aware?"

"You can't tell him from a person," Jack said.

"He's more human than you are," Kit added.

Silver was shaking her head. "That'll all have to be erased. First thing. That's just a waste of processing power. Interferes with the design. You can't have a bomb with feelings."

"Erase him!" Kit sagged back, like something had hit her right in the stomach. "You can't erase Waldo!"

Booker John slammed the bin shut. "And where in the

name of Phobos is this incredible piece of tech? I know
Zeph and Liv didn't get it away from you, or our elec-
trode-decorated friend wouldn't be out here with us." He
pointed at Jack and Kit. "And I searched your suits just
before the torpedo hit." He looked around the room,
scratching his chin. "So, tell me, kiddies. Where is Waldo?"

Behind Booker John, Jack saw the door to the maintenance
bot locker swinging half-open.

Kit flinched. And Jack knew she'd seen the open locker
door, too.

Jack grabbed the edge of the nearest station, to hold himself steady. "He's gone." He shook his head sadly. "We lost him."

SIXTEEN

KIT LOOKED over at Jack, her head tilted.

"You lost it?" Silver's voice reverberated in the small room. "How could you drekking lose it?"

Jack shook his head again. "Out in the Black. There was a radiation wave. It knocked out all the exposed tech." He looked up at Booker John and blinked, then left his eyes wide. The innocent look the customers always fell for. "I was scared and confused. Because I'd never done anything like that before. And the zero gee confused me. I'm not good in zero gee." He sighed, emptying his lungs. "I let go of him. He just slipped out of my hands." He opened his hands, showing them how it had happened. How Waldo had just slipped away.

"It slipped out of your hands!" Silver charged toward him. Jack tried to swim back and away, but she grabbed him by both arms. "Do you know what you've done, you ignorant little spacer? Do you know how much that bot was worth?"

"But," Kit said, "you might be able to still find him. If you leave right away." She moved toward the door, pointing. "We were about thirteen minutes away from the station. He must still be out there in orbit. You should take the *Le Guin.* It's faster. I'm sure you'll be able to find him. Jack and I will wait here." She looked back at him. "Won't we?"

"Sure," Jack said, Silver still clutching his arms. "We'll wait right here."

"Oh," Booker John said. He was shaking his head slowly from side to side. "I could have used you both. Really. The troupe could have used you. Perhaps in a kind of techno *Romeo and Juliet*." He was smiling. "'I was scared. I was confused,'" he said. And he sounded exactly like Jack. "I always knew you were wasted in that pub."

"What the drek are you talking about?" Silver let go of Jack, shoving him so that they both floated away. "We've lost the drekking bot!"

"I don't think we've lost anything. I think the bot is right here." Booker John turned and looked behind him. He opened the door to the bot locker.

"Is there a maintenance problem?" all the bots inside chorused, their optics and antennas fully extended.

"Drekking Phobos." Silver swam over next to Booker John. "You think it's in there?"

"What better place to hide a maintenance bot than with all the other little maintenance bots?" Booker John was peering into the locker.

Silver glared at Jack and Kit over her shoulder. "'Still out there in orbit,'" she said. "Drekking kids." She waved her hand at the bots. "How do we tell which one it is?"

"Well," Booker John said. He tugged at his braid. "I suppose it might answer to its name. Waldo?" he said.

"Is there a maintenance problem?" they all said.

Jack laughed.

Booker John frowned. Then he pointed at Kit. "You must be able to tell. Which one is it?"

Kit shook her head slowly. "It's a standard-model maintenance bot. And they haven't changed the design in over a hundred years. They all look alike to me, too." And she smiled.

Silver leaned into the locker. "Hey!" she shouted. "Hey! You dim bot!"

All the bots juiced their rotors. All the bots surged forward. "Is there a maintenance problem?" they all asked again.

"This is a waste of time," Booker John said. He turned and started opening bins and drawers. "We'll just take them all. The geeks can figure out which is which."

"But no. Wait." Kit's smile dropped away. She started forward. Jack reached for her, to stop her, but she was too far away. "You can't take him. If you meet him. If you talk to him. You can't dismantle him. You'll understand. You can't just erase him." She looked into the locker. "Waldo. Just answer them. Talk to them. Say something!"

"Is there a mainten—"

"Oh, for the love of Calisto, shut up!" Booker John roared. "All of you! Bots, humans. Just shut up." He opened a drawer in the nearest station and pulled out a huge sling bag. "This should do."

"Hurry up," Silver said, nudging him. "Get them loaded."

It took only a couple of minutes to stuff all the bots into the bag.

167

Kit spun back toward Jack. "We have to do something. We can't just let them take him."

Jack raised his hands. Helplessly. What could they do?

"Kid." Silver rubbed an electrode. "You don't get it. We're the good guys here. The people of Pallas need this technology to protect themselves and to force New Oslo and Perseverance to disarm." She looked at Booker John. "Isn't that right?"

"Silver, Silver." Booker John smiled his small, tight-lipped smile. "It's been such an education working with you. True fact." He slung the strap of the bulging bag over his shoulder. He looked like Papa Aphelion. Then he pulled a stun rod out of his pocket. "But if there's one thing I'm not going to miss, it's your rabble-rousing, idiotic cant." And he shot her, point-blank, in the chest.

The whole room filled with an agonizingly bright light. Silver's arms and legs spasmed out, and she flew backward, ramming so hard into Kit that they both came flying toward Jack. He barely managed to scramble out of the way before they hit the back wall.

"Holy . . . holy . . ." Kit's eyes, her mouth, her hands, all were stretched wide in panic. She shoved Silver's body away.

The smell of singed fabric filled the room. Silver hung, head down, above a workstation. Classic dead man's float.

Jack blinked, his eyes hot and stinging. "She's not . . . ? You didn't . . . ?"

"Pluto's sake, I'm an actor. I don't kill people. She should only be out for an hour or so." Booker John looked down at the stun rod. "Unless I've grossly mistaken the charge on this thing."

"Wait a minute." Kit swam forward, around Silver. "Wait a minute. I thought you were partners. I thought you were a bad guy, too."

Booker John looked slightly shocked. "I certainly don't think of myself as a bad guy. But then again, things are rarely so uncomplicated." He adjusted the strap on the sling bag. "The people of Ganymede need this bot more than the people of Pallas do."

"Ganymede?" Jack said.

"Former allies of Perseverance. Alarmed by the current power shift. And when I say 'need,' what I mean, of course, is that they are willing to pay substantially more than the colonists on Pallas." Booker John nodded at Silver. And at Kit. "I told you. They bring all their grudges and their hatreds with them. But if we're smart, we can profit." He grinned, his face lifting in delight. And all of a sudden, he looked just like the old Booker John. Like he was going to lean back and ask for one more glass of whiskey. "Keep your eyes open, Jack. Things are going to get interesting out here in the Black in the next few years."

"But, Booker John," Kit said. "If you met Waldo." She reached toward the bag. Booker John raised his stun rod, and she stopped herself with the edge of a table. "If you just took some time to actually talk to him, I know you'd change your mind," she said. And Jack could tell she was trying to use all those verbal skills. All those social skills. Everything her parents had bought.

"I have to tell you, darling, I find it hard to believe I'd like a sentient bot," Booker John said, and he sounded regretful. "I don't really like most of the *people* I meet." He swung the stun rod from side to side, and Jack held his breath, waiting for the flash. But nothing happened. "But I am, true fact, fond of the two of you. A weakness of my nature, I suppose. So I'm taking the *Le Guin*, but I'm going to leave you the good ship *Niven*. Not fully functional, I'm afraid. I think the pulse torpedo contaminated the mains. But if you keep Arcturus in the scope, you should get back to Freedom eventually." He bent double in a low, sweeping bow. "May flights of angels sing you to your rest." And he swam out into the corridor.

"Wait. Wait." Kit started after him.

Jack grabbed her sleeve and pulled her to a stop. "Don't."

"He's got Waldo!" Her voice was a despairing wail. Tears were puddling in her eyes.

"He's got a stun rod." Jack nodded toward Silver. "And he'll use it." He swam over and stuck his head out into the corridor. The hatch seal warning was flashing, and he could hear the thrum of the air lock starting its cycle.

Jack turned back into the tech lab.

"I should have done something. I promised." The tears had leaked out and were forming a little cloud in front of

Kit's face. "I promised, and I should have done something."

Something rustled behind them.

"Drekking spam." Silver straightened up, rubbing at her chest. "Now that hurt."

Jack swam over to her. "You're awake. He said you'd be out for an hour."

Silver opened the top of her flight suit. "Good thing I paid top credit for this shock vest." She looked up. "First rule of the Black, kids. Never trust anybody. Where'd he go?"

The *Niven* rocked as the portable air lock disengaged. "He's taking your ship," Jack said.

Kit batted away the cloud of tears and swam closer. "But we can go after him, can't we? We can chase him like you chased us."

"The mains are contaminated," Jack said.

Silver rubbed at her chest again. "We'd never catch the *Le Guin*, anyway." She sighed deeply. "Plus, I don't have the access codes to the navigation system. We're going to be lucky to find our way back to Freedom."

"He said to keep Arcturus in the scope."

"Drekking scope." Silver made a face and tapped her electrodes. "I'll try to sweet-talk the computer first." She pushed off and swam into the corridor.

"Drek!" Kit shouted. And she punched Jack in the arm. "Why did you tell her the engines are pranked? She might at least have *tried* to catch him."

"Pluto, I wish you'd stop hitting people," Jack said, rubbing his arm. "I told her about the engines because it doesn't matter. Booker John doesn't have Waldo. Waldo's not in that bag."

The look on Kit's face. He wished he had a recording wafer. "Then where is he?" she shouted.

"I'm here," Waldo said.

Kit whirled. Waldo was hovering in the doorway to the pod garage.

"Waldo!" She swam over and grabbed him. And then she kissed him. Right between his optics. "I thought Booker John took you. I thought you were going to be chopped up for parts."

"I knew the storage was the first place they'd look," Waldo said. "I hid in the pod."

Kit looked back at Jack. "But how did you know? When they opened that locker, all the bots looked alike. I couldn't tell them apart."

Except that Waldo had that little dull place, on his right antenna, where he was always scratching. "There were thirty-two when Waldo first opened the storage. And there were still just thirty-two when Booker John filled the bag. So I knew he wasn't in there."

Kit's face cleared, and she laughed. "The numbers thing."

"Right." Jack looked at Waldo. "The numbers thing."

And Waldo was looking back at him, the optics twitching just a little.

Kit shook her head. "Imagine the look on Booker John's face when he finds out he doesn't have the right bot." She laughed again, louder.

"Just be glad Ganymede is on the other side of the Asteroid Belt," Jack said. He glanced back at the open door. "And you might want to lower your voice. We still have to hide Waldo from Silver until we get back to Freedom."

"No one has to hide me," Waldo said.

"What are you talking about?" Kit said. "Of course we have to hide you." Her eyes were getting big and bright again. "Unless we took the pod. We can go—" She stopped.

"We don't have to get to Seattle Prime anymore, Kit," Waldo said, gently. "Silver was lying. There is no one there who can help us."

Kit looked at Jack. "There must be somewhere. There must be somewhere out here where he'd be safe." She waved her hand. "You're always saying how big it is out here."

"I think," Jack said slowly, "the best thing right now would be to go back to Freedom and figure out what to do next. We'll just have to figure out a whole new plan."

"Jack's right, Kit," Waldo said. "You should go back to Freedom." He juiced his rotors and hovered over one of the workstations. "But I'm not going back with you." He opened a drawer with a pincer. "I'm leaving in the escape pod."

SEVENTEEN

"YOU'RE LEAVING in the escape pod?" Kit said. Like Waldo was making one of his jokes. One of his bad jokes. And she didn't get it. She looked at Jack.

He shook his head. He didn't get it either.

Waldo looked up from the drawer. "Once the geeks on Ganymede discover that none of those bots is me, don't you think they're going to come looking? Don't you think Booker John will come looking? Or someone like him? Don't you think there'll always be someone from Ceres or Beijing II or one of the other Earth colonies looking for me?" He pointed an extended pincer. "I'm not going to live like that."

"Waldo. We can think of a plan," Kit said.

"Kit." Waldo's voice was much softer. "You can't hide me forever. And you can't spend your life worrying about me. I'm not going to let you live your life like that." He bent over the drawer and pulled out some laser blades. "I've made up my mind."

Jack could tell he meant it. And in a dim sort of glitched way, he understood what Waldo meant. Jack opened a drawer. Shut it. "He'll come after her, you know." He looked at Waldo. Not at Kit. "Booker John. He'll just think she's hiding you again."

"I've already thought of that." The optics swiveled toward him. "I'm going to ping the *Le Guin* when it's closer to Ganymede. I'm going to make it clear Kit doesn't have me. It will be safer that way. For everyone." The optics didn't twitch, didn't waver.

"But then Booker John will just come after you!" Kit shouted.

"Well, he can come after me," Waldo said, "but he won't find me. No one will find me."

"And where, exactly, do you think you can go in that escape pod where no one will find you?" Kit was floating with her legs straight, her hands on her hips.

"The pod should have enough fuel to get me deep into the Belt. Maybe even farther." Waldo was opening more drawers. Pulling more stuff out. Servos, power packs, wafers were floating all around him. "The chances of anyone finding me if I don't want to be found are astronomically small."

Jack nodded. It was a true fact. You could hide millions of escape pods out in the Black. "He's right," he said.

Kit glared at him. "You don't have to encourage him."

"I'm not encouraging him. I'm just saying he's right."

"Once I'm established, I'll be able to set up my lab," Waldo said.

"Lab?" Kit sounded like she'd never heard the word before. "What lab?"

"I did a lot of thinking about this. When I was in the pod." Waldo was pulling memory components out of another drawer.

175

"You were in there for, like, ten minutes," Kit said.

"I can think quite a bit in ten minutes, Kit," Waldo said. "And I realized that no one knows Dad's research better than I do." He looked up from a storage bin. "I'm going to try to duplicate his work. I'm going to try to make more bots like me." His voice shook a little. Like he was excited, but trying to hide it.

"You're going to make *what?*" Kit said.

Jack laughed, partly at the way Kit said it, and partly because he could imagine it. He could imagine a whole bunch of bots. Just like Waldo. He laughed again. "A bot colony."

"Exactly." Waldo buzzed. And Jack knew he was imagining it, too. "I can download all my own programs. Study them. And then try to replicate the patterns. But I need more bots." One optic looked at Jack. "I need all the bots you can find."

"Right." Jack started pulling himself around the room, opening lockers, cupboards, bins, drawers.

"But some of the work—some of the enhanced intelligence —took Dad years and years to develop," Kit said.

"I have years and years, Kit. I have all the time in the solar system." Waldo sighed. "Maybe even more."

Kit groaned. "This is the single most dysfunctional thing I've ever heard." She put her hands on either side of her head, like it ached. Like she was trying to hold something in.

Jack had found a bunch of bots. A cam, a vac, a couple of wipers. The drawer of the front workstation was full of tiny drivers. He held some up. "Are these too small?"

Waldo clicked a couple of times. "I'm not sure. But I'll take them. I'll try anything."

Kit dropped her hands. "I'm coming with you," she said. In her "I'm right, so don't argue with me" voice.

Waldo was focusing on a tool drawer. "Don't be ridiculous, Kit. You'd just take up space. And there's no way I could afford the resources. I'm dumping all the water, the food. I'll need the atmo, of course, for my rotors." He stopped and looked at her. He pulled in everything except for his antennas and his optics. "I will miss you, Kit. True fact. You're my family, and I'll miss you more than . . . well, more than I can imagine. And I can imagine immense amounts." His optics drooped. "But I have to do this alone."

Kit swam over closer to Jack. "You live out here. You're a spacer. Tell him this won't work. Tell him this is cracked!"

Waldo was looking at him, too.

Jack looked down. He couldn't tell Waldo to go. And he couldn't tell him to stay. He couldn't think of anything to say, to either one of them. He pulled open a bin. "Hey. Hey. Look at this." He held up another maintenance bot. All its ports were sealed tight. "It must be pranked, or it would have been with the others."

Waldo flew over and extended a probe to connect with the bot. He looked at Jack. "It's just a glitching rotor." And he buzzed, long and loud. "This is cosmic, Jack. True fact! I have a far greater chance of success with something so much like me."

Kit yanked the bot out of Jack's hands. "And then what are you going to do? When you're orbiting around out there with a bunch of feeling and thinking and talking wipers and vacs and cams? What are you going to do?"

Waldo scratched at his antenna. "Maybe even the pod itself." He gestured with the other probe. "You know, if I can augment the computers on the pod, I could have a sentient spacecraft. The applications for deep-space exploration would be incredible. We could be the first emissaries from Earth to distant worlds." And he sounded excited and happy and maybe even a little bit scared.

"A diplomat," Jack said. And he laughed. "You'd be good at that, Waldo."

"Oh, for the love of Persephone," Kit said.

Waldo shrugged. "Of course, I'll have to discuss it with the other bots. We'll have to decide together." He clicked again. And then he hovered closer to Kit. Gently, he extended a probe and rested it on her cheek. "Once I'm settled, I should be able to establish some contact. I'll ping you, first chance I get. And one day, I might be able to see you again. Or you might come visit me."

Kit didn't answer.

"Kit," Jack said softly. And he put his hand on her arm. He could feel her shaking, through the thin fabric of her sleeve. "He's going to be a lot safer than he would be on Freedom. Or anywhere else." He looked at Waldo, then back at Kit. "I bet, you know, I bet your dad would think so, too.

I bet your dad would think this is a good idea."

Kit was staring down, like there was something really, really interesting on the floor. Like she couldn't stand to look at either one of them. It was so quiet, Jack could hear the atmo scrubbers again.

Finally Kit looked up again. Her face was scrunched up. "So. Okay. Don't just float there. Let's get these drekking bots into the drekking pod."

It took them only about twenty minutes to search and strip the entire tech lab. And then Jack went to the galley and the crew quarters. He found two more vac bots and some scrubbers and a vid player.

When the pod was loaded, Waldo looked around at all the bots, the tools, the spare components. He whistled softly. "Stellar."

Jack pointed at him. "Don't forget to check the solar report."

Waldo buzzed. "I will definitely check the solar report."

"And once you're settled, ping Freedom." Jack held out his hand. "But remember to conceal your identifier."

"I will." Waldo rested his right probe in Jack's hand. "Thank you for all your help, Jack. Meeting you has been one of my best experiences. I've acquired a lot of data from you."

"Yeah," Jack said. "Yeah. Me too. I've acquired a lot of data too."

And he left Kit and Waldo alone in the garage.

He swam on out of the tech lab and out of the cargo bay

and into the corridor. And then he swam down to the galley.

Booker John had been right. The bins were full of nutricubes. And there were fresh water pouches in the coolers.

He ate a cube. It wasn't half bad. Wasn't half good, either, of course.

The ship shuddered, slightly, as the escape pod released.

Jack ate another cube. Kit swam into the galley.

And Silver's voice shrieked out of the comm. "What the drek just happened? Computer says an empty pod was released!"

Kit keyed the comm call. "It was an accident."

"I didn't think that button did anything," Jack added.

"Well, don't touch anything else! Drekking kids." Silver clicked off.

"I really, really don't like that woman," Kit said. She took a deep shuddery breath. Her eyes were bright green.

"Yeah." Jack shrugged. "The two of us together, I'll bet we could put her out the air lock." He tried a smile.

"Let's get back to Freedom first," Kit said. "We can do it then." She wasn't smiling. He wasn't sure if she was joking. "This is so toxic." Her eyes squinched up, holding in the tears.

"It is. Totally toxic."

"He's just been a big pain. From the moment Dad first activated him. He's been nothing but a big pain."

Jack nodded. He held out a water pouch.

She took it. "And you know, he was always wanting to see something, to do something. He'd never just sit in one place. If he'd stayed with me, someone would have caught him for sure."

"Absolutely."

He put his hand on her head. Her hair was soft. She smelled of sweat. And something spicy. Sort of like the rice at Kumar's.

Then he swam back to the bin and got a handful of cubes. He let them go, and they floated slowly out around him.

Kit sniffed, once, loudly, and pushed her free hand through her hair. "We've got to come up with a story."

Jack ate a cube. "A story?"

"For when we get to Freedom?" She snagged another cube. "How are you going to explain to Gert where you've been?"

If they got the engines going. If they found the right quadrant. It would still take several hours to get back. Jack sighed. "I don't know. The last thing she said to me was, 'Don't do anything I wouldn't do.'"

For a few seconds, they just looked at each other. And Then, together, they started laughing.

Jack put back his head, and his body turned in a slow, easy somersault. "Gert'll get over it. I'll just be scrubbing cook pots for a while." Gert would be easy. But Fast Marco . . . Fast Marco was going to be tougher.

And Annie. Jack shook his head, imagining how he was going to explain all this to Annie. He got out a water pouch. Annie would be okay, too. Eventually.

Kit popped a cube into her mouth. "I'll help you pay for the scooter."

Jack took a small sip of water. "You staying on Freedom?"

"I want to be there, if Waldo pings me."

"*When* he pings you," Jack said.

She nodded. "*When* he pings me. Besides, it's much cheaper for the Company to employ me on Freedom than to send me all the way back to Earth. Don't you think?"

"Probably. You could present them with a cost analysis." He took another sip of water. "I'll help you run the numbers."

"Hey." Silver's voice squawked through the comm. "Does either one of you know how to use a scope?"

Jack and Kit looked at each other. She keyed the comm call. "Jack does."

"Then get up here." Silver clicked off.

Kit frowned at the comm. "I suppose we have to help her."

Jack finished off the water and dropped the pouch in the recycler. "If she's lost, so are we. If you want to get back to Freedom and start finding a job, we'd better help her."

"I thought you were leaving. I thought you were going to Liberty Station." Kit fingered one of the cubes, like there was something really interesting stuck on it.

"Oh. Yeah. Liberty." He'd forgotten all about it. The new job. His mother's brother. And his kids. "Cousins," Annie had called them.

He had his passage booked on the *Asimov*. Away from

Freedom. Away from Gert. And Fast Marco. Rigel and Nguyen and Amalthea and Leo.

Annie.

And now Kit.

She looked up from the cube, her eyebrows arching up.

He'd even miss Waldo's ping. When it came.

"I've got forty-three days," he said. "Before I have to decide." Jack swam for the door and glanced back. "You coming up to the bridge?"

She scooped up a handful of cubes. "Of course. I've got skills, too, you know, spacer."

"Oh, yeah," Jack said. He grinned. "I know. You're not half-bad. For a rat."